# PAYBACK

Latham looked at Fargo with renewed interest, his eyes narrowing. "Fargo, is it? Your first name wouldn't happen to be Skye, would it?"

"It is, in fact," Corporal Worthington confirmed.

Kline had been listening with rapt attention, and now he moved next to Latham.

"Did I hear right? This is him?"

"Appears so," Latham said.

"Are you goin' to stop me?" Kline asked.

"I am not."

Kline faced the Ovaro, his face hardening. "Does my handle mean anything to you, mister?"

"Should it?" Fargo said.

"You killed a cousin of mine a year or so back," Kline snarled. "I've been hopin' I'd run into you someday so I could do to you like you did to him." And with that, Kline leveled his rifle.

# THE TRAILSMAN

#394

# BURNING
# BULLETS

by

## Jon Sharpe

A SIGNET BOOK

SIGNET
Published by the Penguin Group
Penguin Group (USA) LLC, 375 Hudson Street,
New York, New York 10014

USA | Canada | UK | Ireland | Australia | New Zealand | India | South Africa | China
penguin.com
A Penguin Random House Company

First published by Signet, an imprint of New American Library,
a division of Penguin Group (USA) LLC

First Printing, August 2014

The first chapter of this book appeared in *Six-Gun Inferno*, the three hundred ninety-third volume in this series.

Copyright © Penguin Group (USA), LLC, 2014

 REGISTERED TRADEMARK—MARCA REGISTRADA

ISBN 978-0-451-46805-5

Printed in the United States of America
10  9  8  7  6  5  4  3  2  1

# The Trailsman

Beginnings . . . they bend the tree and they mark the man. Skye Fargo was born when he was eighteen. Terror was his midwife, vengeance his first cry. Killing spawned Skye Fargo, ruthless, cold-blooded murder. Out of the acrid smoke of gunpowder still hanging in the air, he rose, cried out a promise never forgotten.

The Trailsman they began to call him all across the West: searcher, scout, hunter, the man who could see where others only looked, his skills for hire but not his soul, the man who lived each day to the fullest, yet trailed each tomorrow. Skye Fargo, the Trailsman, the seeker who could take the wildness of a land and the wanting of a woman and make them his own.

*1861, the Flathead Lake country—where a tinderbox of hate ignited an inferno of violence.*

# 1

The patrol was weeks out of Fort Laramie when they stopped for the night beside a creek that had no name. They'd finished their meal of hardtack and beans and were relaxing after their hard day on the trail. It was then, as they sat talking and joking, and some smoked their pipes, that the trouble started.

Skye Fargo saw it coming. A bigger man than most, broad at the shoulders and narrow at the hips, he wore buckskins that had seen a lot of use. So had the Colt on his hip.

Fargo was under orders to guide the patrol to the Flathead Lake country. He'd been there before. Fact was, his wanderlust had taken him most everywhere west of the Mississippi River, which was why he was so widely regarded as one of the best scouts on the frontier.

Private Gunther didn't think so. Gunther was bigger than Fargo, with a square slab of a face and enough muscle for an ox. He was of the opinion that he was the toughest trooper in the U.S. Army and made a point of showing how tough he was by beating any and all comers. The problem was, he didn't wait for them to come to him. He went after them.

Gunther had been needling Fargo whenever and however he could. It had started at Fort Laramie when the colonel announced that Captain Benson would be leading a patrol and that Fargo was to be their scout. The men were standing at ease at the time on the parade ground, and Gunther had made bold to loudly remark that he hoped Fargo could find where they were going. No one laughed. Hardly anyone ever laughed at Gunther's jokes. He didn't care. He wasn't trying to be funny. He had issued a challenge.

That became clearer as the days passed. Fargo lost count of the comments Gunther made. They were never outright insults. Gunther was too smart for that.

But they were as close as a man could come to fighting words, such as on their second day out. Fargo had been riding down the

1

line when Gunther loudly declared to the private next to him, "For a scout, he sure does sit a saddle poorly. Look at how he flops around."

Everyone knew Fargo was a superb horseman. It was the troopers, many of whom had seldom sat a saddle, who bounced and flounced and clung to their saddle horns when the going got rough.

Fargo had let the remark pass. He'd let others pass, too. The time when Gunther had said, "I hear tell our scout has lived with redskins. Makes you wonder whose side he's on, doesn't it?" And the time when Gunther had remarked, "How come our scout gets to have a shiny new repeater, and we have to use single-shot rifles?"

Along about the tenth night, Captain Benson had walked over to where Fargo sat and squatted. "I'm in a quandary over Private Gunther."

Fargo had tried to recollect if he knew what a "quandary" was.

"I've told him twice now to leave you be, but he persists with his foolish antics. I can send him back to the fort, but that seems extreme. Especially since I'd have to send a couple of others with him, for protection's sake."

Fargo had grunted.

"So I ask you—what do *you* want me to do?"

"Nothing."

"He'll just keep at you. You heard about the fight he had with Bear River Tom, didn't you?"

Fargo had indeed. Bear River Tom was another scout and one of his close friends. The fight took place in a saloon when Gunther remarked that given Bear River Tom's well-known fondness for tits, it was a shame Tom hadn't been born female, so he could have tits of his own. Tom didn't think that was funny and hit Gunther with a chair. They went at it, but a lieutenant broke up their fight.

"You're not saying much," Captain Benson now said. "But then, you never do."

He glanced over at where his troopers were jawing. "The army has more than its share of troublemakers, I'm sorry to say. Bullies are all too common."

Fargo liked Benson. The captain had enough experience to be competent and was firm but fair with those under him. "Let me handle it. And don't butt in when it comes to blows."

2

"If I let it go that far, I'll have to put him on report once we get back. It's a matter of maintaining discipline, you understand."

That was where they'd left it. Then, that very evening as they were unsaddling their mounts, Private Gunther had looked over at Fargo stripping the Ovaro and laughed.

"Will you look at that critter? It's about the most sorry excuse for a horse I ever did see."

Once again, no one laughed.

And this time Fargo refused to let it pass. He bided his time until after their evening meal, when Gunther stretched and yawned and said, "Another day in the saddle tomorrow, boys. I hope our scout's ass can take it. He's moving a bit stiff these days."

Fargo set down his tin cup and stood. Hooking his thumbs in his gun belt, he stepped around the fire and planted himself in front of Gunther. "Speaking of asses, when are you going to get your head out of yours?"

The other troopers froze.

"What was that?" Gunther said.

"You're the biggest ass at the post, so I reckon there's plenty of room for that swelled head, but still."

"You can't talk to me like that."

"As for my horse," Fargo went on, "it can ride rings around any animal in the army any day of the week. Not that I'd expect a horse's ass like you to know a good horse from a sorry one. That takes brains. And yours keep leaking out your ears." He paused. "That is what that brown stuff is?"

Gunther colored red from his collar to his hat.

Most of the soldiers looked at Captain Benson, expecting him to do something.

Private Gunther glanced at Benson, too, and seemed puzzled.

"Yes, sir, boys," Fargo said to the rest, "when it comes to asses, Gunther here is the top of the heap."

Pushing to his feet with his cup of coffee in his hand, Gunther glowered. "That's mighty brave talk when you know the captain won't let me take a poke at you."

Fargo glanced at Benson. "Captain?"

"Poke away," Benson said.

Gunther's mouth curled in a smirk. "Well, now. Ain't this something? Most officers would be telling me to behave myself."

"You'll behave starting tomorrow," Fargo said.

"Why will that be?"

3

"Because your jaw will be too swollen for you to talk and the rest of you will hurt like hell."

Gunther laughed. "Listen to you." He balled his left fist and held it up. "I've busted boards with this."

"Boards don't fight back."

Gunther gazed at the other troopers, eating up the attention. Puffing out his chest, he said, "Place your bets, boys. But if you bet on him, you'll lose."

"No betting," Captain Benson said. "No gambling allowed."

"But you'll let me take a swing at him?" Gunther asked uncertainly.

"I'm not *letting* you," Captain Benson said. "I'm just not *stopping* you. There's a difference."

"Damned if I can see what it is," Gunther said, adding sarcastically, "sir."

"Are you done flapping your gums?" Fargo said. "We don't have all night."

Gunther pointed at Fargo's holster. "No using that. I hear you're slick as hell with a six-shooter and I'm no gun hand."

Fargo pried at his buckle. "What you are," he said, "is all mouth."

Some of the soldiers laughed.

As for Gunther, he watched Fargo set the gun belt to one side, and when Fargo straightened, he threw his coffee in Fargo's face.

## 2

Fargo was expecting Gunther to try something. Bullies nearly always fought dirty. He'd seen how Gunther was holding the tin cup down at his side, as if trying to hide it.

So when Gunther flung the coffee at his face, he got his arm up in time to keep the coffee out of his eyes.

Gunther seized the advantage by tackling him around the waist.

Fargo had figured the big trooper would use his fists. But no, Gunther was a grappler. Fargo winced as he was slammed to the

4

ground and his hat went flying. Gunther tried to knee him, but he shifted and took it on his thigh. He rammed a fist at Gunther's chin and winced a second time. Gunther had a jaw like an anvil.

Gunther butted his forehead at Fargo's face. Fargo jerked aside and tried to heave Gunther off, but it was like trying to toss an ox. Gunther must weigh two hundred and fifty, if not more.

Snarling in frustration, Gunther went for a headlock. Fargo twisted, slipped his head free, and flung an arm around Gunther's neck. If Gunther wanted to wrestle, fine. Fargo was no stranger to it.

They rolled, each seeking to fasten a grip the other couldn't break.

The other troopers were yelling. Fargo didn't catch much of it, but it seemed that most were rooting for him.

An elbow jab to the gut forced Fargo to focus. He retaliated with an elbow to the temple that appeared to hurt him more than it did Gunther, whose skull must be as thick as a buffalo's.

After a sudden move, Gunther was behind Fargo, his arms encircling Fargo's waist. "Got you now," he rasped in Fargo's ear, and squeezed.

It was like being caught in a vise. Fargo felt as if his stomach and intestines were about to burst. Fargo thrashed and clawed at Gunther's arms but couldn't free himself. Clamping his hands onto one of Gunther's, he applied all his strength to forcing it from his body. Gunther resisted for all of half a minute, until Fargo got hold of his thumb and was on the verge of snapping it.

Gunther broke away and rose to his knees.

Fargo did the same. He had no time to set himself. Gunther pounced, seeking to apply a neck hold. Fargo ducked, gripped Gunther's wrist, and levered Gunther's arm up and around, slipping behind him as he did. Gunther cried out and reached over his shoulder with his other hand, trying to gouge Fargo's eyes. Fargo wrenched on the arm and Gunther cursed and bucked. Quickly, Fargo reached under Gunther's other arm, gripped it above the elbow, and pulled it back while simultaneously bracing his elbow against the small of Gunther's back.

"Ready to give up?"

"Like hell."

Gunther exploded. Whipping his legs up, he hooked them around Fargo's head and twisted, apparently seeking to break Fargo's neck. Fargo pulled his head free but lost skin in the process.

Gunther drove a knee at Fargo's face. Skipping back out of reach, Fargo crouched.

Confidence lit Gunther's brutal features. "You're not so tough, scout. I can take you."

Fargo coiled and said nothing.

"The great Skye Fargo. The best scout alive. The one everybody is afraid of," Gunther taunted. "I knew you were hot air. And once I've licked you, everyone else will know it, too."

Captain Benson chose that moment to unexpectedly ask, "Do you want me to stop it?"

"No," Fargo said.

"I'm going to tie you into a knot and break a few bones," Gunther boasted. "Just see if I don't."

"Anytime you're ready, jackass."

Gunther sprang. He flung his arms wide, trying for a bear hug. With his great strength, he could easily crush a man's ribs.

Fargo had other ideas. He knocked one of Gunther's arms aside and tripped him.

As Gunther went down, Fargo slammed onto Gunther's back, slipped his right foot under so that it was around Gunther's leg, and grabbed both of Gunther's wrists.

Gunther howled. He bucked, but Fargo's leg around his prevented him from rising more than an inch or two off the ground. Bunching his shoulder muscles, Gunther sought to tear his arms loose.

Fargo wrenched, pulling both arms back as far as they would go, and then some.

Gunther cried out. "You're tearing them from their sockets."

Fargo wrenched harder.

A shriek tore from Gunther's throat. His chin dipped to his chest, and he closed his eyes and groaned.

"Want me to do it again?" Fargo asked.

Spittle dribbled from a corner of Gunther's mouth.

"I can't hear you."

"No," Gunther gasped.

"Say it louder."

"No, damn you," Gunther said. "I don't want you to do it again. I'm licked, all right?"

"Say it louder."

"I'm licked!" Gunther shouted, and his entire body went limp in defeat. "Happy now?"

Fargo rose and stepped back. "You brought it on yourself."

Gunther nodded bleakly. "You're one tough bastard. I shouldn't have prodded you like I did."

"It wasn't that, so much," Fargo said.

Gunther looked up in confusion. "Then what got your dander up?"

"You insulted my horse, you stupid son of a bitch."

# 3

Over the next several days Private Gunther was as meek as a kitten. He didn't insult anyone. He went about his duties quietly, and slowly. He could barely move his arms. Whether riding or walking, he held them close to his sides to lessen the constant pain.

Fargo put Gunther from his mind. He had more important concerns. The patrol was passing through Blackfoot territory, and the Blackfeet had held a grudge against whites since the days of the Lewis and Clark Expedition. Lewis and another man had killed two warriors who had been trying to steal their guns. It didn't help matters that whites then gave guns and horses to the Nez Perce and the Shoshones, longtime enemies of the Blackfeet.

Since then, the Blackfeet had simmered with hostility. They resented any and all white intrusions. So far there hadn't been an uprising, but that was mainly because their territory was so far from anywhere that few whites ventured there. Trappers and ore hounds, for the most part, until recently.

Word had reached the army of a party of settlers who were homesteading in the mountains to the west of what was known as Flathead Lake. That could cause problems with the Flatheads, a friendly tribe granted their own reservation years ago. The army wanted to be sure the settlers weren't on Flathead land, and if they were, evict them.

So here Fargo was, guiding two dozen troopers over some of

the most rugged terrain on the continent. Few of them had ever been this far out from civilization. Only two, Captain Benson and Sergeant McKinney, had fought hostiles. To say that Fargo didn't have much confidence in the new recruits was an understatement. Still, he had a job to do.

The fifth morning after his clash with Gunther, Fargo began to breathe a little easier. They were entering Flathead territory and were less likely to encounter Blackfeet.

Fargo was tightening the cinch on the Ovaro when Sergeant McKinney came over. A model of soldiery, he carried himself ramrod straight. His uniform never had a blemish; his boots were always shined.

"The captain's regards. He'd like you to go on ahead and scout out the lay of the land."

Fargo liked McKinney. The only real soldier among the enlisted men, the sergeant was the glue that held the patrol together. "I aimed to do that anyway."

Sergeant McKinney nodded. "The captain's regards again. He remembers the smoke from yesterday and was hoping you would investigate."

The day before, after the sun had gone down and the gray of twilight was giving way to the black of night, a sentry called out that he'd spotted smoke in the distance. Fargo had gone over with some of the others but hadn't seen any smoke. "A dollar says Private Timmons was seeing things."

"No betting, remember?" Sergeant McKinney grinned, then shrugged. "Could be Flatheads." He sobered and said, "Could be Blackfeet."

"Could be a whorehouse but I doubt it."

McKinney laughed. "You and your doves. Bear River Tom once told me that you have the worst case of tit fever's he's ever seen."

"Tom's a fine one to talk. He hasn't stopped talking about them since he was weaned."

"Granted," McKinney said. "But back to the smoke. I could send a couple of troopers with you."

Fargo finished with the cinch. "No."

"They're not all worthless," McKinney said. "I've trained them, haven't I? Some show real promise."

"It's still no."

"How about Corporal Worthington, then? He's young, but he listens well, and he's a damn fine shot."

Fargo gripped the reins and reached the saddle horn, about to mount. "I don't need my hand held."

Sergeant McKinney shook his head. "You've got it all wrong. No one knows better than me that you're the best there is at what you do. I'd like some of it to rub off."

"How's that again?"

McKinney nodded at the troopers, who were preparing to head out. "A day with you can teach them more than parade ground drills for a year. It'll be something they can brag to their friends about. Riding scout with the Trailsman."

"You're laying it on a little thick."

"That's what folks call you these days, isn't it? And I'm not laying it on so much as asking a favor. Share some of that wood-lore and whatnot you have in that head of yours."

"Damn you, Mike."

"I know," McKinney said. "It's a lot to ask. The army hires you to scout, not to wet-nurse. But consider this. The things the corporal picks up from you could mean the difference for a lot of good men living or dying someday."

Fargo sighed. "I'll take Corporal Worthington."

"And two or three others?"

"Worthington and only Worthington. You want me to take others, I will another time."

"Good." Sergeant McKinney smiled. "Worthington shows real promise. I'd like to see him make sergeant one day. You're helping me a lot. I can't thank you enough."

"You can thank me by buying me a bottle when we get back."

"A whole bottle? You sure you don't want me to treat you to a dove while I'm at it?"

"Now that you mention it . . ."

"A bottle for Worthington, and if you take one or two others out sometime, I'll throw in a whore."

"Deal," Fargo said.

"I'll go fetch him. And remember, I want him to learn about tracking and such. Not about cards or women or whiskey."

"Well, damn," Fargo said.

Corporal Worthington was a cherub in uniform. He had curly blond hair and blue eyes and a baby face. He was also on the plump side, a remarkable feat given the quality of army food. Beaming fit to split his jaw, he came over leading his horse and snapped to attention. "Sergeant McKinney says I'm to accompany you, sir."

Fargo reminded himself that McKinney thought the boy showed promise. "First off, you don't call me sir. Save that for the officers."

"Sorry. I just want to make a good impression."

"You can impress me more if you don't stand there as if you have a broom shoved up your backside."

"But I'm a soldier, si—" Corporal Worthington caught himself. "When we're drilling we always have to stand straight."

"You're not drilling now," Fargo said. "Act around me like you do around your friends when you're at ease."

"Oh, I couldn't do that, Mr. Fargo."

"I'm not a 'mister,' either. And why the hell not?"

"Why, as famous as you are, it wouldn't be right."

"Famous, my ass."

"But you are. Everyone has heard of you. Word is that you've fought the Apaches and the Sioux and all kinds of hostiles." The corporal lowered his voice. "They also say you're powerful fond of tits."

"That's Bear River Tom, not me."

"You're not fond of them?" Corporal Worthington said in surprise.

Fargo inadvertently raised his voice. "I'm not powerful fond of tits, no."

The rest of the patrol stopped what they were doing to stare. Even Captain Benson and Sergeant McKinney.

"Son of a bitch," Fargo said.

"The one thing no one told me," Corporal Worthington said, "was how much you cuss."

# 4

Fargo was still annoyed half an hour later. He didn't mind helping Sergeant McKinney. But every time he glanced at Corporal Worthington's eager babyish face, he couldn't help thinking this was a mistake.

They were crossing the tail end of a range overlooking the long valley that was home to Flathead Lake. Thick forest covered every slope, phalanxes of ponderosa pine broken here and there by stands of cedar, spruce, and aspens. Firs were common, higher up.

Wildlife was everywhere. Blue jays screeched and black-billed magpies winged about. Now and again ravens flew overhead, the rhythmic beating of their wings loud in the rarefied air. Hawks pinwheeled in search of prey. Eagles soared on the high currents, both the bald and the golden variety.

Deer were abundant. So were elk, but the elk stayed better hidden. A few times, Fargo caught the white flash of mountain sheep on towering crags. He found sign of buffalo, too.

Fargo had about forgotten about Corporal Worthington when he happened to look over and the corporal was gazing in wonder at a pair of sparrows frolicking in a bush. "Sparrows, for God's sake," he muttered.

Corporal Worthington tore his eyes from the birds. "Pardon? You need to speak up, sir."

"What did I tell you about that sir business?" Fargo nodded at the bush. "What's so interesting about them?"

"I'm from New York," Worthington said.

"They don't have sparrows there?"

"New York City," the corporal amended.

"None there, either?"

"It's not the kind," Worthington said, and motioned at the rolling vista of woodland and peaks. "It's being *here*. In the Rocky Mountains. Seeing things hardly anyone has ever seen before."

"If we counted all the folks who have seen sparrows," Fargo said, "we'd run out of numbers."

"No, you don't understand. In the city I hardly ever saw wild things. Not even sparrows. Here, creatures are all around us. Everywhere we look. That butterfly a while ago. That doe and her fawn. The hawks. The eagle."

"You get used to them," Fargo said.

"You, maybe. Sure, sparrows are ordinary. But here they're part of the wonder of it all."

"You, sound more like one of those poets than a soldier. Don't get carried away. Out here there's a dark side to things that can get you killed."

"I'm not stupid."

Fargo wasn't quite sure what he was, and decided to find out. It would be good to know more about him should they wind up at the wrong end of a gun or a charging grizzly. "How old are you, anyhow?"

"What's my age have to do with it?"

"How old?"

"Eighteen," Worthington said, quickly adding, "but I'll be nineteen in a month."

"What are you doing in the army?"

"Ever since I can remember, I've wanted to be a soldier. To wear a uniform. Some might say that's not much of a dream, but it was mine."

"And here you are." It impressed Fargo, the boy going after something he wanted so much. A lot of folks didn't have that gumption. "Is it all you'd thought it would be?"

"Frankly, no," Worthington said. "I'm not fond of being told what to do. I'm not fond of drilling on horseback for an hour and a half a day, six days a week. Or of all the marching around we have to do. And don't get me started on the food."

Fargo chuckled.

"But you know what? God help me, I love it. I love serving my country. I love that I can make a difference."

"At what?"

"At making the frontier safe for folks to live. That's the reason we're here. To protect people. To put down hostiles when they act up. Those sorts of things."

"The hostiles don't see you that way," Fargo mentioned. "To them, whites are invaders who want to take their land away."

"I've thought about that," Corporal Worthington said as he

12

reined around a spruce. "And do you know what I think? I agree with them."

"You do?" Fargo said in considerable surprise. A lot of people, settlers and soldiers alike, believed it was their manifest destiny, as some called it, to lay claim to all the land between the Mississippi River and the Pacific Ocean.

"Some of these tribes have lived where they do for more years than any of them can remember. The land is their home. So of course they resent it when we move in and say it's ours."

"The Blackfeet would be pleased to hear you say that."

"Probably not," Worthington said. "Because even though I think it's wrong, it's right."

"I've lost your trail," Fargo said.

"The East is bulging with people. In some states, all the good land has been taken. And game has grown so scarce families can't keep food on the table." Worthington gestured at the panorama of wilderness that stretched in all directions as far as the eye could see. "Out here there's a feast of plenty. Game everywhere. Good land to be had. Everything a man can want to make something of himself."

"And the Indians?"

"They have a right to live here, but they can't keep it all to themselves. The way I see it, the two sides should try to get along. Work things out so that both can live in peace."

Fargo grunted. He understood Worthington better now. And he liked what he'd learned. "Those are fine sentiments, Corporal. But there's one thing you'd better keep in mind if you want to live to old age."

"What's that?"

"A lot of folks don't want to get along. A lot of whites kill Indians just because they're red and a lot of Indians kill whites because they're not red. The land has nothing to do with it. They kill out of hate, plain and simple."

"Killing another person over his skin color is wrong. I don't care what anybody says."

Fargo agreed. "As fair-minded as you are, I reckon you'd make a good sergeant someday. Maybe even an officer."

"Why, thank you," Worthington said, and he actually blushed. "I've thought about that, as a matter of fact."

They came around a bend in a slope, and Fargo stiffened. "Sergeant McKinney wants me to teach you some of what I know, so I'll start with two things that can save your life."

"I'm listening."

"The first is to never take it for granted that others think the way you do. Trust too easily and you could wind up with a bullet or an arrow in your back."

"And the second thing?"

"Slide that rifle of yours out of your saddle scabbard and hold it in front of you, casual-like."

"Whatever for?"

"In about a minute or two," Fargo said, "someone might try to kill us."

# 5

The corporal had been so caught up in their talk he hadn't noticed smoke rising from a hollow below. Fargo had spied it right away. He'd also glimpsed the glint of metal in a cluster of pines near where the smoke came from. Now, winding down the slope, he switched his reins to his left hand and placed his right hand on his hip above his Colt.

It could be anyone. Anyone white. Indian war parties had more sense than to let their campfires give them away.

Fargo figured it might be some of the settlers. Then again, he never took *anything* for granted.

Worthington slid his rifle free and cradled it. He kept glancing every which way, and his throat bobbed.

"Calm yourself, Corporal," Fargo said quietly. "Nerves are no good in a fight."

"What's out there? Hostiles?"

"You haven't seen the smoke yet?" Fargo could smell it.

Worthington peered ahead, and blinked. "I'll be. Sergeant Mc-Kinney is always telling us we need to be more aware of things."

Figures moved in the pines. Two or three. Fargo saw hats and a vest. That none of them had taken a shot at the corporal and him was encouraging, but as soon as he came within pistol range, he drew rein.

Worthington followed suit.

"Let me do the talking. Don't shoot unless I do."

"Yes, sir."

Fargo squared his shoulders. "You in the trees. Come out where we can see you." When no one answered, he added, "If you don't, as soon as the rest of the patrol gets here, we'll come in and find you. They're not far behind." He mentioned that last in case they took it into their heads to open fire. The shots would bring the soldiers right quick.

A man called out, "How do we know you're with the army? You could be makin' it up."

Fargo pointed at Corporal Worthington. "What's he wearing, you damn lunkhead? A dress?"

"Oh," the man said. "A uniform."

"Your eyes work," Fargo said. "Does your brain?"

"Give us a minute to talk it over."

Fargo didn't see what they needed to talk about. "Don't keep me waiting too long."

"Why do you talk to them like that?" Corporal Worthington whispered. "It'll make them mad."

"I can't abide stupid."

"People can't help being how they are."

Fargo didn't reply. He sat and waited impatiently, and presently another man joined those already there and after a brief exchange, not two or three but five men came cautiously into the open, all with rifles. His instincts kicked in. Their looks, the way they carried themselves—these were wolves, not sheep.

The man who had just joined the others wasn't much over five feet tall. He wore a black hat and had a Smith & Wesson on his left hip. Cradling a Spencer, he sauntered to a stop. He raked Fargo from hat to boots and then looked at Corporal Worthington, and smirked. "On you it should be, boy."

"I beg your pardon?" Worthington said.

"I heard what this scout said," the man replied. "You're too young to be much of a soldier."

"My sergeant says I have the makings of a good one."

"Does he, now?"

Fargo wished the corporal had kept his mouth shut. Now the five knew he was next to harmless. Or would be in a fight.

15

"Hell, boy," the man in the black hat went on, "with all that fuzz on your chin, you don't even shave yet. Some soldier you are."

"I happen to be a corporal."

"Good for you," the man said. "I've never been fond of blue-coats myself. Most are weak sisters pretendin' to be men."

"How about me?" Fargo intervened. "Think I'm weak?"

The man lost his smirk. A wary look came into his dark eyes and he shook his head. "No, mister. You're the real article."

The others focused on Fargo, too. A tall one with stubble on his chin and a cheek bulging with chaw spat juice, wiped his mouth with his sleeve, and remarked, "You're one of them fancy-pants scouts."

"Did you figure that out by yourself or did someone have to tell you?" Fargo said.

Bristling, the tall one took a step. "Be careful how you talk to me. I don't like to be insulted."

"Then you shouldn't be so stupid. You were the one who didn't know a uniform when you saw one."

"Go to hell."

"Simmer down, Kline," the short man in the black hat said.

"You heard him, Latham. He called me dumb when I ain't."

Latham glanced at the tall one. "Do I have to tell you twice?"

Shaking his head, Kline said quickly, "No. No need. I didn't mean nothin' by it. Honest."

That told Fargo a lot, right there. Latham was top wolf in this pack, and dangerous. Even his own pards feared him. "You keep your pups in line, I see," he remarked.

"And I see what you're doin'," Latham said. "You're goadin' us. Takin' our measure."

The short man was smart, too, Fargo realized.

Corporal Worthington cleared his throat. "What are you gentlemen doing here, if you don't mind my asking?"

"Gentlemen?" Latham said, and snorted. "Can't you tell, General? We're settlers, lookin' for a place to homestead."

To Fargo's amazement, the boy took him seriously.

"Why here, of all places? You'd be safer down near Fort Laramie, where the army can protect you."

"Did you hear that, fellas?" Latham said to the others. "The army wants to protect us."

Several laughed.

"We've heard there are settlers up this way," Corporal Worthington said. "It's why the colonel sent us."

"How many did he send, exactly?" Latham asked.

"Twenty-four," Corporal Worthington answered. "Well, twenty-six if you count the captain and Mr. Fargo here."

The information produced a lot of scowls. It also caused Latham to look at Fargo with renewed interest, his eyes narrowing. "Fargo, is it? Your first name wouldn't happen to be Skye, would it?"

"It is, in fact," Corporal Worthington confirmed.

Kline had been listening with rapt attention, and now he moved next to Latham.

"Did I hear right? This is him?"

"Appears so," Latham said.

"Are you goin' to stop me?" Kline asked.

"I am not."

Kline faced the Ovaro, his face hardening. "Does my handle mean anything to you, mister?"

"Should it?" Fargo said.

"You killed a cousin of mine a year or so back," Kline snarled. "I've been hopin' I'd run into you someday so I could do to you like you did to him." And with that, Kline leveled his rifle.

# 6

In the wilds a man learned to react quickly, or else. When a bear charged, you shot quickly and thought about the shooting after the fact. When a rattlesnake was about to bite, you shot by instinct and prayed your aim was true.

It was the same now. Fargo didn't think. He acted. His hand flicked to his holster and he had the Colt out and fired a split instant before Kline could squeeze the trigger. The lead struck Kline in the shoulder, jolting him half around. Kline cried out and his rifle clattered to the ground. Clutching himself, he doubled over.

The others froze.

All except for Latham. He looked at Kline and then at Fargo, and he did an unexpected thing: He smiled. "You're not the only one who can take an hombre's measure."

"What?" Corporal Worthington said, sounding stunned. "What was that?"

Fargo swung his Colt to cover a filthy man in a beaver hat who had started to raise a Sharps. "Try and you die."

The filthy man hesitated.

"Don't," Latham said.

"No?" the filthy man said.

"You heard me, didn't you, Hagler?"

"I heard you." Hagler let the barrel dip.

Latham turned back to Fargo. "That wasn't a favor. It's just not the time or the place."

Kline had fallen to a knee and was groaning, blood dribbling between the fingers pressed to his shoulder. "I hurt, Latham. I hurt bad."

Latham walked over, gripped Kline's wrist, and pulled the hand away. He peered at the wound; then without any forewarning, he struck Kline across the face. "Quit your blubberin'. You can be a damn infant sometimes." He jabbed a finger into the wound, and Kline cried out. "The slug went clean through. You'll bleed a bit and be good as new in a week or two."

Kline opened his mouth as if to say something but apparently thought better of it and clamped his mouth shut again.

"See? You can be a man if you try." Latham faced Fargo and the corporal. "Now, where were we?"

"You were claiming to be settlers," Fargo said.

"Wait," Worthington interrupted. "Mr. Latham, aren't you going to bandage your friend?"

"I'm a mister now?" Latham said, and laughed. "No, boy, I'm not. He got himself shot. He can bandage himself, or get one of the others to do it, although they likely feel the same as I do."

"Why, that's downright cruel," Worthington said.

"Life is cruel, pup. Anyone who tells you different has their head in the clouds." Latham pursed his lips and scratched his chin. "And you know what? This palaver is gettin' us nowhere. My pards and me are leavin'. Give my regards to your captain. Tell him if he's smart, he'll turn around and take all you little boys in blue back to Fort Laramie."

"Hold on," Corporal Worthington said. "I'm not so sure I should let you leave."

"You can't stop us."

"I can," Fargo said. He was still holding his Colt pointed squarely at Latham.

Latham didn't bat an eye. "Could be you can," he said, nodding. "Could be you're quick enough to gun all five of us, although I have my doubts. But no way in hell are you quick enough to gun all seven."

"Seven?" Corporal Worthington said.

Latham motioned at the pines. "You can count, can't you, boy? Or don't they teach sums and such to bluecoats these days?"

Two men with rifles were half-hidden in shadows. They had the rifles aimed and were plainly waiting word to shoot.

Fargo swore under his breath.

"Always have an ace in the hole, that's my motto," Latham said, and chuckled. "It's how I've lasted so long at what I do."

"Settling, you mean?" Fargo said.

Latham laughed. "I do a heap of that." He motioned at the others, and they walked off, Latham strutting like the cock of the walk.

Kline was the last to go. He had to try twice to stand, and paused to glare at Fargo. "Don't think you've seen the last of me, you son of a bitch. You killed my cousin and now you've put lead in me."

"Through you," Fargo said.

Kline's jaw twitched. "We'll meet again, and when we do, it'll end different. Mark my words."

"I believe you," Fargo said.

"You do?"

Fargo nodded. "Next time, I'll shoot you in the head."

Kline was anything but amused. He trailed after the others, dripping blood with every step.

"You sure like to provoke people," Corporal Worthington said.

Fargo began reloading. "You can tell a lot about a man by how he provokes."

"Those men aren't settlers, are they?"

"Do you really need to ask?"

"What do we do? They shouldn't be here. Captain Benson will want to talk to them."

"He might get his chance yet." Fargo finished, twirled the Colt into his holster, and leaned on his saddle horn.

The seven hard cases were moving deeper into the pines. Just before Latham disappeared, he looked back and gave a cheery little wave.

"Rub it in," Fargo said.

"I beg your pardon?" Corporal Worthington said. "Rub what in?"

"We should push on." Fargo reined to the north and clucked to the Ovaro. They would reach Flathead Lake in an hour or so. Beyond that was the valley where real settlers were supposed to have their homesteads.

Corporal Worthington kept fidgeting in his saddle and looking back. Finally he coughed and said, "Can I ask a question?"

"Sergeant McKinney wants me to teach you," Fargo said.

"Is that a yes?"

"Ask your damn question."

"All right, I will." Worthington took a nervous breath. "How did I do back there? Be honest with me?"

"You were pitiful."

"That's awful harsh."

"You asked." Fargo was beginning to regret bringing the young trooper along.

"What did I do that was so awful? I thought I conducted myself fairly well, all things considered."

"You were too nice, too friendly. You should have seen right away that they were curly wolves."

"I'm not any good at reading people, I'm afraid."

"You'd better learn," Fargo advised, "or you won't live long enough to make sergeant."

# 7

Flathead Lake had the distinction of being the largest body of freshwater in the western half of the United States. The early beaver trappers called it Salish Lake, after the tribe that claimed it as part of their territory. When the mountain men who came along later started calling the Salish "Flatheads," the name of the lake was changed to Flathead Lake.

Fargo drew rein a stone's throw from the water's edge and announced, "We'll wait here for Captain Benson."

"I hope he can find us," Corporal Worthington said.

"You saw me blaze trees and leave sign," Fargo reminded him. "They'll be here before nightfall."

Worthington gazed along the shore. "Are we on Flathead land now, or is this still Blackfoot country?"

"We're at the south end of Flathead territory. That doesn't mean we won't run into Blackfeet, so keep your eyes skinned."

The blue expanse of the lake seemed to stretch an interminable distance. The wind was stirring whitecaps, and here and there ducks and geese swam.

"How far to the other side?" Corporal Worthington asked.

"About thirty miles, give or take," Fargo said as he dismounted. "The widest point is about fifteen."

"Good Lord. That's what, pretty near two hundred square miles? It would take a week to go all the way around." Worthington alighted stiffly and shook his left leg. "How deep is it?"

"I haven't swum to the bottom lately."

"I was serious."

"So am I. How the hell would I know? Go ask a fish."

Worthington shook his other leg. "Is the water safe to drink?"

"It hasn't killed the Flatheads and they've been drinking it for a hundred years or better."

"I was only asking."

"You ask a lot." Fargo led the Ovaro over so it could drink. Hunkering, he cupped some water and sipped.

Corporal Worthington followed his example. Sinking to his knees, he went to lower his own hand.

"Better be careful," Fargo said.

"Eh?" Worthington looked around. "Of what? All I see is that mallard."

"Of the monster," Fargo said.

"You're pulling my leg, trying to scare me. There's no such thing."

"As God is my witness," Fargo said. "The Flatheads say there's something in this lake. Something that comes to the surface from time to time. Something so big it capsizes their canoes."

"Damn me if I don't think you're telling the truth."

"Did you just cuss?" Fargo said, and chuckled. "Being around me has done you some good, after all."

"Do you believe the Flatheads? Have you seen the monster with your own eyes?"

"I'm not one of those who brands Indians as liars because they're not the same color as me," Fargo said. "And I did see . . . something . . . once. But don't ask me what it was."

"I'd love to see it, whatever it is," Worthington said excitedly. "It would be something to tell my kids about one day."

"Seeing a big fish?"

"Not just any fish," Worthington insisted. "I'll call it the Flat-head Monster. How does that sound?"

Fargo shrugged. "I doubt the name will catch on."

Corporal Worthington drank, wiped his hand on his pants, and stood. Squinting against the glare of the afternoon sun, he asked, "Does this monster of yours have bumps?"

"Not that the Flatheads have mentioned," Fargo said. "Although there was a warrior who claimed it had horns." He looked up. "Why?"

"Because I'd swear there's a big fish heading right toward us," Corporal Worthington said, "and it has bumps."

"What?" Fargo stood and shielded his eyes with his hand. "That's a canoe, you idiot. Those bumps are heads."

"Oh," Worthington said. "Are they Flatheads or Blackfeet?"

"They're not close enough to tell yet." Fargo turned and shucked the Henry from its saddle scabbard. "Just in case," he said, levering a round into the chamber.

The "bumps" acquired shoulders and became the upper bodies of four warriors paddling in smooth strokes. It was obvious the warriors had spotted them and were coming to investigate.

"What do I do?" Corporal Worthington asked.

"Stay calm," Fargo said.

"I've never talked to Indians before. How do I do it?"

"You use your mouth."

"No. I mean, how will you communicate? Do you speak their tongue? Or do you know sign language?"

"What good would a scout be who doesn't know sign?" Fargo answered more gruffly than he intended. The boy's constant questions were irritating him.

"Can you teach me some? When you have the time."

"How about right now?" Fargo closed his right hand and held it just under his right shoulder, then lowered it several inches. Next he placed the tips of the fingers of his right hand on his mouth and bobbed his head.

"That was sign language?" Corporal Worthington said excitedly. "What did you say?"

"Shut up."

"Oh." Worthington frowned. "See what I mean about you being mean? Would it have hurt you to ask nicely? Maybe throw in a 'please'?"

"Are you a lady of the night in a tight red dress?"

"What? No."

"Then you don't get a 'please.' "

"Hardy-har-har."

Fargo grinned. Actually the two signs he'd used had been "remain" and "silent," which was as close as sign language came to telling someone to quit yapping.

The canoe was a lot closer. Close enough to see that the warriors weren't wearing war paint. At a gesture from the man in the bow, they stopped paddling and stared.

"What are they doing?" Worthington asked.

"The same thing Latham did," Fargo said. "Taking our measure. And before you ask, they're Flatheads." Leaning his Henry against his leg, he clasped both hands in front of him, the back of his left hand to the ground, the sign for peace.

"Are you telling them to shut up, too?" Corporal Worthington asked, and laughed at his little jest.

"They haven't said anything yet."

Worthington shook his rifle. "You're making me mad. All you do is tease me."

"Now you've done it," Fargo said.

"Done what?"

"The Flatheads are leaving."

The warriors were using their paddles to turn the canoe. Once they did, the man in the stern kept an eye on Fargo and the corporal as the canoe made off the way they had come.

"What did I do that they're going away?" Worthington asked. "Was it when I shook my rifle at you? Why would that make them leave?"

"They didn't know you were shaking it at me."

"Give a yell and let them know."

"Give a yell in sign language?"

"Well, darn," Corporal Worthington said.

23

"You wouldn't happen to have a flask in your saddlebags, would you?"

"Of course not. Liquor isn't permitted in the field. I'd find myself up on charges. Why do you ask?"

"I could use a drink."

"How come?"

Skye Fargo sighed.

# 8

The troopers and their cavalry mounts were caked with dust and weary from their long day of hard travel when, late in the afternoon, they reached the clearing Fargo had chosen for their camp. It was on a shelf that overlooked Flathead Lake. A breeze off the water brought refreshing coolness after the heat of the summer's day.

The canoe never returned. Fargo had told Corporal Worthington to climb a tree and stay up there scanning the lake for the Flatheads. But the real reason was that Fargo wanted some peace and quiet.

Not that he was worried about the Flatheads. The tribe had proven remarkably peaceful. They'd never, to his knowledge, attacked a single white. The Blackfeet, on the other hand, wouldn't hesitate to swoop down on a couple of whites or an entire patrol if there were enough warriors in the attacking party.

Fargo had kindled a fire and put a pot of coffee on when the patrol clattered out of the trees.

Captain Benson swiped at the dust on his sleeve and grinned. "A man of leisure, I see."

"Did you have any trouble following my trail?" Fargo asked. He'd expected them an hour ago.

It was Sergeant McKinney who answered, "Only at the end, the last mile or so, when there weren't any marks."

Fargo sat up. "The hell you say."

"You left the usual signs?" Captain Benson asked. "We didn't come across any of the usual blazed trees or rocks pointing the way."

Corporal Worthington had shinnied from the tree when he saw them coming, and now he piped up with "Fargo marked the trail as always, sir. I saw him with my own eyes."

"What could have happened?" Captain Benson wondered as he dismounted.

"I might have an idea," Fargo said, and explained about his encounter with the seven so-called settlers.

"Latham, Kline, and Hagler were three of their names, you say?" Captain Benson said thoughtfully when Fargo finished. "About a month ago the colonel received word that a wild bunch led by a man called Latham had drifted up our way. Apparently this gang caused no end of trouble down to Texas. The Rangers got after them and they lit out."

"The Texas Rangers have put fear into a lot of bad men, sir," Sergeant McKinney remarked.

"That they have," Fargo agreed. The Rangers were some of the toughest lawmen anywhere. They had to be. Texas outlaws weren't weak sisters. And now seven of them were in Flathead country.

"Are you suggesting," Captain Benson said, "that these outlaws are responsible for the missing marks?"

"They knew a patrol was on its way and weren't happy about it," Fargo related. "It would have been easy for them to find the rocks I left and scatter them. They could have removed the blaze marks, too."

"To what purpose?"

"Men like that, what are they doing here?" Fargo rejoined.

Benson shrugged. "Outlaws wander where they will."

"But why *here*?"

"I don't get what you're driving at."

"I do, sir," Sergeant McKinney said. "What would bring a man like this Latham to Indian country? It certainly wouldn't be the Indians. They hardly have anything worth stealing." He gazed to the northwest. "But rumors about a lot of new homesteaders might."

"Green apples for the plucking," Fargo said.

"I'll be damned," Captain Benson declared. "All the more reason we must find these settlers as quickly as possible."

"I'll start searching west of the lake tomorrow," Fargo said.

"Whoever they are, they should've checked in with the colonel before they came all this way. Settlers are always homesteading where they shouldn't and causing no end of problems for us."

"What will you do when we find them, sir?" Sergeant McKinney asked.

"I can request that they leave, but I can't force them to unless they're on Flathead land. Even then, if they refuse, I can't take arms against civilians."

"Maybe they won't resist, sir," Corporal Worthington said. "Maybe they'll have respect for our uniforms and for the government and do as you ask without giving us a hard time."

Fargo, Captain Benson, and Sergeant McKinney looked at him.

"What?" Corporal Worthington asked.

"Oh, to be so young again," Captain Benson said.

"Go join the men, Corporal," Sergeant McKinney directed. "Tell them I'll be over in a few minutes and to prepare to bed down for the night."

Puzzled, Worthington walked off.

"He's a good trooper, but he's another green apple," Captain Benson said. "He has too much faith in his fellow man."

"I told him the same thing," Fargo mentioned.

"Is that wrong of him, sir?" Sergeant McKinney asked.

"When it clouds his judgment, yes," Captain Benson said. "If these homesteaders have had time to build their cabins and settle in—and our information suggests they have—they're not about to meekly give their new homes up just because I ask them to."

"But there are the Blackfeet, and now these outlaws, and God knows what else," Sergeant McKinney said. "If they don't listen, they could die."

"There's that," Captain Benson said.

# 9

Fargo intended to head out at first light, and was up before most of the troopers. His breakfast consisted of three cups of piping-hot coffee. He saddled the Ovaro, talked briefly with Benson, and was under way as golden rays illumined the horizon.

He stuck to the west shore of Flathead Lake. The going was easier than in the timber. He saw fish leap, saw ducks and mergansers and a few loons. Once several Canada geese winged overhead.

Fargo expected to come on a Flathead village sooner or later. This time of year, bands came to the lake to enjoy summer's bounty. But when he spied smoke, he leaped to the conclusion it must be the outlaws, and rode faster.

A rise overlooked their camp. From amid pines, Fargo counted six men, backwoods sorts in homespun. Four were relaxing around their big fire. The other two, who were considerably younger and might have been sons of some of the others, had cast lines in the lake and were fishing.

Rifles and shotguns had been carelessly left lying about, hardly any in easy reach.

"Infants," Fargo muttered, and gigged the Ovaro. He rode slowly so they would see him coming and not mistake him for an Indian and start shooting. He'd been told that from a distance, with his buckskins and bronzed tan, he could pass for one. Sure, he had a beard, but some people weren't as eagle-eyed as others.

Amazingly he got within twenty yards before a lanky man with straw hair thrust out an arm and hollered, "Lookee there! Someone is comin'!"

A mad scramble for guns ensued. Even the fishermen set down their poles to run for their rifles.

As Fargo drew rein, he found himself staring down gun muzzles. "You can relax. I'm friendly," he said with a smile.

"How do we know that?" the lanky man demanded.

"I bet he's one of them, Rufus," a stocky barrel of a man in a coonskin cap said.

"We should shoot him off that horse," declared a third.

"What the hell?" Fargo said.

The oldest, who had gray hair at the temples, lowered his shotgun. "Let's not be hasty, boys."

"He has to be one of them, Granville," Rufus said. "Who else would be in this neck of the woods?"

"He does look mean," the stocky barrel said. "I say we put lead in him and stomp on his corpse."

"Do you ever listen to yourself, Vernon?" Granville said. "We're not stompin' on no corpse 'less'n we have proof. And he don't look to be one of them to me."

"One of who?" Fargo asked, but was ignored.

"Explain to me your thinkin', brother," Vernon said to Granville.

"Take a good gander. Did Lester say any of them wore buckskins? He did not. He was clear what they were wearin', Lester was."

"Maybe this one changed clothes," Vernon said.

"That must be it!" Rufus exclaimed. "He changed, thinkin' he could trick us."

"And then he was dumb enough to ride right up to us by his lonesome?" Granville said.

Vernon and Rufus looked at each other and Vernon said, "Well, that would be sort of feebleminded."

Fargo didn't like that some of them were still pointing their rifles. "Are you idiots done?"

"What did you just call us?" Rufus said.

"You build a fire that could bring every Blackfoot and Piegan from here to Canada. You sit around with your heads up your asses and don't even post a lookout. And you talk about shooting a man when you don't know who he is." Fargo shook his head in disgust. "If that's not being idiots, it's as close as they come."

"He has a point," Granville said.

"Lower those damn rifles," Fargo snapped.

"Why should we?" Vernon said. "How do we know we can trust you? We've already had one of us shot."

"That's right," said a man with a sorrowful expression and ears a hound dog would envy. "We tracked the varmints this far but lost the sign."

Fargo had had enough. One instant his hand was empty. The next his Colt was out and cocked. "I won't tell you gents twice."

"Land sakes!" Rufus blurted. "Did you see that?"

"I didn't see nothin'," Vernon said. "He got it out too quick."

Granville did a brave thing. He stepped between Fargo and the others, in effect blocking their muzzles with his body. "Do as he says. I don't like guns pointed at me, neither."

"We're takin' an awful chance," the sad-eyed man said.

"I trust my instincts, Solomon," Granville said. "And mine tell me he's not out to do us harm. Think about it. He could have shot us from ambush, easy as pie. Instead he rode in to say howdy."

"Well," Vernon said sourly, but he lowered his shotgun.

"You sure are quick, mister," Rufus complimented Fargo. "I wish I was as quick like you. I always wanted to be, but I came out of my ma's womb slow and have been slow ever since."

"What?" Fargo wasn't sure he'd heard right.

The one called Granville smiled. "I'm sorry we weren't friendlier, but we're a mite jumpy. One of our homesteads was attacked." He nodded at the Colt. "You can put your six-shooter away. None of us will try to do you harm."

Fargo deliberately twirled the Colt forward a few times and then reversed the spin and slid it into his holster.

Rufus whistled. "Dang my ma, anyhow. Why couldn't she have made me quicker?"

"Where'd you learn to use a pistol like that, mister?" Vernon asked.

"You strike me as bein' one of them gun hands," Solomon said. "We've heard about some who are as slick as you, but we ain't got any down to Tennessee. Not many in the hills use pistols."

"Mostly we shoot with rifles," Rufus said. "Shotguns, too, but they're mainly for close up, and for ducks and whatnot."

"We ain't none of us got our own revolvers," Vernon said. "I wouldn't mind havin' one, but our wives would call it a terrible waste of money."

"And the last thing I want is my missus mad at me," Rufus said. "She's cantankerous enough when it ain't even her time of the month."

"I hear that, brother," Solomon said. "When my wife is on the warpath, I hide in the outhouse."

"And people wonder why I'm not married," Fargo muttered.

Granville motioned at their campfire. "Why don't you light

and set a spell, mister, and we can become better acquainted? I'd like to hear who you are and what you're doin' hereabouts."

Fargo would like to learn about them, too. But something had occurred to him. These were hill folk. And hill folks were notorious for liking something that he liked just about more than anything. "Before we do, you wouldn't happen to have any whiskey, would you?"

"As a matter of fact, we do," Granville said. "But it's a little early in the day yet, don't you reckon?"

"Not if you're really thirsty," Fargo said.

# 10

They were hill folk from Tennessee and as friendly as could be. Five families "with a heap of kids," as Rufus put it.

"It got so crowded back there," Granville explained, "we couldn't take it anymore."

Rufus nodded. "You couldn't hardly spit without hittin' your neighbor."

"I had some not a mile from my place," Vernon said. "When the wind was right I could hear his missus singin' to her hogs."

"That's peculiar," Solomon said. "Who sings to hogs? Cows I can understand. Singin' to them makes them give sweeter milk. But hogs? What's that do? Make sweeter ham?"

"Now, that would be somethin'," Rufus said. "Ham is about the best food there is, if you don't count puddin'."

"How's that 'shine goin' down?" Granville asked Fargo.

"Fine," Fargo said, and coughed. They'd brewed it themselves back in the hills, and it kicked harder than a mule. "Go on about why you came all this way." He took another swallow and swore it burned clear down to his toes.

"Well, it got crowded, like we were sayin'," Granville said, "and game was gettin' mighty scarce."

"That it was," Vernon said. "Used to be, I'd hardly step into the woods and there'd be deer or a grouse or a bear to shoot. But it got so I had to hunt half the day to fill the supper pot."

"And who wants to work that hard at anything?" Rufus said. "A man's got better things to do than work."

Granville took up the account. "We'd heard tales about the West. About how there's more land than anybody can shake a stick at. About how there's so much game a body can't hardly turn around without seein' somethin' to shoot."

"So we talked it over," Solomon said, "and held a family meetin' and took a vote as to whether we'd come west or not."

"We even asked the wives how they felt," Vernon said. "Even though women ain't got the right to vote for presidents and such yet."

"Most everybody was for it, so we packed up and here we are," Rufus said.

"Back up a bit," Fargo said. "How did you travel? By Conestoga?" That's what most did, but he hadn't seen any sign of wagon tracks.

"Who can afford one?" Granville said. "We're not rich. We rode here and toted our effects on pack mules."

"What about your furniture? Your stoves? Your beds?"

"We took the beds and the tables apart and brought them in pieces," Granville said. "And none of us had stoves."

"We're fond of fireplaces," Vernon said.

"I'd like to see somebody tote a stove on a mule," Rufus said. "That would be plumb comical."

"Your wives and children didn't mind riding all this way?"

"It was only ridin'," Granville said. "What's to complain about?"

"Why Flathead country? You could have settled anywhere."

"We asked the sutler down to Fort Laramie which Injuns were the friendliest and he said the Flatheads. Then he told us about this here lake, and how it's almost as a big as an ocean, and we figured that'd be a sight to see."

"Sounded to us like right pretty country," Vernon said. "And we wouldn't have to worry about our hair."

"So we held another meetin'," Granville said. "The women-folk were eager to have a roof over their heads. They said that if we didn't find someplace soon, they'd turn around and head back to Tennessee, and us menfolk could be hanged."

"Contrary females," Rufus muttered. "They sure get uppity when they want their own way. Me, I never let mine boss me around."

"I don't know as I can blame them for wantin' to find a place," Vernon said. "We'd been ridin' for months. That's hard on the backside."

"Not mine," Rufus said. "I've got me a backside as hard as a rock. I can ride for a month of Sundays and it doesn't bother me a lick."

"Which one of you was attacked by the outlaws?" Fargo wanted to know.

"None of us," Granville said. "It was our cousin, Lester. He couldn't come on account of he was shot."

"It's not that serious, though," Rufus said. "He's breathin' all right."

"So there are five homesteads?"

Granville nodded. "Mine, Vernon's, Rufus's, Solomon's, and Lester's. Countin' the wives and all the kids, there are over fifty of us."

"I could count the exact number, but I'd have to take off my shoes," Rufus said.

"You touch your feet and your woman will complain about the stink," Vernon said. "Mine always does."

"Which is plumb silly," Rufus said. "Foot stink can't be helped."

Fargo drained his cup and held it out for more. Maybe it was the whiskey, but what they were saying didn't seem half as ridiculous as it had earlier. "Tell me more about the attack."

Granville answered, "Lester and his family were set on just as the sun was goin' down. The outlaws figured to take 'em by surprise, but Lester's oldest gal, Periwinkle, saw them sneakin' up and let out a yell, and the next thing, Lester and his missus and most of their nine kids were swappin' lead with the varmints."

"Nine kids?" Fargo said in amazement.

"They ain't kittens," Granville said, and some of the others laughed. "We believe in big families. I have eleven sprouts my own self. Vernon has twelve. Rufus there has us all beat with fourteen."

"My missus likes her pokes," Rufus declared proudly.

"You're lucky," Solomon said. "My missus didn't want but six kids and when we had number seven she about caved in my skull with a rock. And don't even ask me how riled she got over number eight."

"That's women for you," Rufus said. "They treat their wombs like they was their wombs alone."

"Females can be silly," Solomon agreed.

"I'd like to see this valley of yours," Fargo told them. He didn't explain why. For the time being he preferred to keep the news about the cavalry to himself. "If you have no objections," he added tactfully.

"Shucks, we don't mind," Granville said. "Now that we know you're not one of them outlaws, you're more than welcome."

"Just remember one thing," Vernon said. "No triflin' with our women. We have some pretty daughters and we expect you to behave around them."

"Can you do that?" Rufus demanded.

"I can sure try," Fargo said.

## 11

The Southerners called it Tennessee Valley. As heavily timbered as the surrounding slopes, it had appealed to them because of the abundance of game.

With the typical industry of backwoodsmen, they'd cleared five sites for their cabins and within a couple of months of their arrival, each family had a cabin of its own.

"We have plans for this here valley," Granville said as they neared the first of the homesteads, which happened to be his. "Give us another year and we'll have ground cleared for vegetable gardens for the women. And some of us aim to bring in cows and maybe a few hogs."

"No hogs for me," Vernon said. "I'd rather have chickens. At least chickens lay eggs."

"You can have hogs and chickens, both," Granville said.

"I want some hogs," Rufus said. "So I can have ham on occasion. Have I mentioned how much I like ham?"

"It's as good as pudding," Fargo recollected.

33

"Why, yes, it is. You and me have the same taste buds," Rufus said.

A horde of kids of all ages were running and skipping and frolicking in front of the cabin. When one shouted and pointed, a stout woman with her hair in a bun appeared in the doorway, a wooden bowl on her hip and a large wooden spoon in her hand.

"That's my woman," Granville said. "A fine figure of a gal, is she not?"

"That's some spoon she has," Fargo said.

Stumps dotted the clearing, along with holes where a few stumps had been dug out.

"We still have a lot of clearin' to do," Granville mentioned. "I hope to have most of it done before winter hits."

"Don't forget to stock up plenty of firewood," Fargo advised them.

"How's that?" Rufus asked.

"Winters here are harsh. The snow can drift higher than that cabin. And the temperature can drop to twenty below."

"Below what?" Rufus said.

"Zero."

Rufus looked at Granville. "Is that cold?"

"It will freeze your pecker off."

"Well, damn. I'm fond of my pecker."

"Not only that," Fargo continued, "but a blizzard could sock you in for a month or more."

At that they chortled, and Solomon said, "That was a good one, mister. There ain't that much snow in all the world."

"I mean it," Fargo said.

"Sure you do," Rufus said. "There's no place that sees that much cold and snow, except maybe the North Pole. How dumb do you reckon we are?"

"Any chance I could have more whiskey?" Fargo asked.

"Not with the missus lookin' on," Granville said. "Later on we can sneak out. I have some hid where she won't find it."

"Too bad," Fargo said.

"You're commencin' to worry me," Granville said. "You've already had more liquor before noon than I have in a whole day. You're not one of them fellas who can't go without, are you?"

"I have my moments," Fargo said.

"Well, you'll just have to do without. Our women won't like it if you walk around tipsy."

"You don't want to rile our women," Vernon said.

Rufus nodded. "I'd rather stick my head in a bear's mouth than have my wife mad at me. At least the bear kills you quick."

"God," Fargo said.

"Don't be blasphemin', neither," Granville warned him. "Our women take powerful stock in the Scriptures. When we're at the table we say grace, and at night the sprouts say their prayers."

"My Etta makes me say prayers with ours when we tuck them in," Rufus mentioned.

"I thought you didn't let her boss you around," Vernon said.

"I don't. That's not so much her bossin' me as it is tellin' me what to do."

No sooner did they draw rein than Granville's brood swarmed him. He joshed and laughed and hugged each one, even the boys who looked to be sixteen or older. Then it turned serious and they besieged him with questions.

"Did you catch those varmints that shot Lester, Pa?"

"Is it true they're honest-to-goodness outlaws?"

"Will you hang 'em for what they done?" a boy of about ten asked. "I can help if you do. I'm good at knots."

Just then the stout matron emerged, still carrying her bowl and her spoon. "That's enough pesterin' your pa. Can't you see he's brought company? Scat and get to your chores or there will be sore backsides tonight."

"Ah, Ma," one said.

"We were just askin'," said another.

They dutifully trudged off, and presently Fargo was pumping a female hand as strong as any man's.

"This here is my Charlotte," Granville introduced her, "the apple of my eye."

"Oh, hush," Charlotte said, blushing.

"Her and me been hitched pretty near thirty years now," Granville said.

"Thirty-four," Charlotte corrected him.

Behind her someone coughed.

Charlotte looked over her shoulder. "Oh. Where did you come from, child? I thought you were sweepin' the cabin. Here, meet our visitor." She moved aside.

The "child" had to be in her early twenties. Lustrous blond hair cascaded past her slender shoulders, framing an oval face with piercing green eyes, high cheekbones, and ruby lips. She wore a simple homespun dress, which did little to hide the swell of her full bosom or the sweep of her thighs.

"I almost forgot about you, gal," Granville said, and laughed. "Fargo, this here is my oldest, Darlene. She takes after her ma, don't you think?"

Fargo felt himself stir, low down.

"Pleased to meet you," Darlene said in as husky a female voice as he had ever heard. She held out her hand.

Fargo enclosed it in his, and a lightning bolt shot down his spine. He grew hot all over.

"Are you all right, mister?" Darlene asked. "You look poorly all of a sudden."

"It's all that liquor he drank," Rufus remarked thoughtlessly. "I never saw anybody drink so much so early in the day."

"Oh my," Charlotte said. "You're a drinkin' man?"

"Don't start on him," Granville said. "I'm a drinkin' man myself."

"Just so he doesn't get carried away," Charlotte said. "You'll behave yourself while you're under our roof, won't you, Mr. Fargo?"

Fargo couldn't take his eyes off Darlene. "I'll be a paragon of virtue."

"What's a paragon?" Rufus asked.

"It means he won't do any wrong," Granville said.

"That's nice of him," Rufus said.

Fargo wished he hadn't said that. It was an outright lie. When it came to virtue, particularly where women and whiskey were concerned, his wouldn't fill a thimble.

Darlene didn't help matters by saying, "I've never met a paragon before. This should be interestin'." And she smiled ever so sweetly.

# 12

Since they had a guest, Charlotte insisted on "whippin' up a mess of stew," as she put it. Fargo told her not to bother on his account, but she refused to listen. "It ain't often we have company, mister. Not from outside the family. We should do it right."

The other men didn't stay to eat. They were eager to reach their own cabins.

Granville mentioned he would see them again when he escorted Fargo to Lester's place.

Fargo wasn't in any hurry. He could report back to Captain Benson whenever he wanted. Plus, there was Darlene. He noticed that she glanced at him a lot as she went about helping her mother prepare the stew. It showed she was interested, and he was hopeful it would lead to more.

Granville sat across from him at their long table and talked about the move from Tennessee, and how fine it was not to be hemmed in by too many neighbors anymore.

"What about Vernon and Rufus and the others?" Fargo brought up. "From what you've told me, they don't live that far away."

"Kin don't count," Granville said. "If we were all livin' fifty feet from each other, we wouldn't mind. A body can never have enough family around."

Granville sure had a passel of his own. The kids were everywhere, buzzing about like so many bees. The only time they quieted and sat still was when Charlotte said grace.

The stew was delicious. Usually Fargo didn't eat at midday, but he had two bowls and coffee, besides.

Darlene sat two chairs down from him, and every now and then she would casually gaze in his direction and make it a point to catch his eye.

Fargo was even more encouraged.

The family was about done eating when Granville announced,

"Fargo here would like to have a talk with Lester about that attack on his place. We're leavin' in a bit."

"What's your interest, Mr. Fargo? If you won't mind my askin'." Charlotte said.

"From the sounds of things, I tangled with the same bunch," Fargo said. He was still debating whether to tell them about the army patrol. He wasn't sure how they'd take the news, and didn't want to upset them, as nice as they'd been.

"This is the first you've mentioned that you had a run-in with those varmints, too," Granville said.

"I was hunting them when I ran into you," Fargo fibbed.

The whole family saw Granville and him off, smiling and waving as if they'd be gone ages. Darlene stood with her left arm across her middle just below her breasts, waving, staring only at Fargo.

"A fine brood you have there," Fargo remarked, imagining how Darlene would look without that dress.

"Ain't it, though?" Granville said happily. "My pa always said that a man can be dirt-poor when it comes to money but rich as can be when it comes to family."

Fargo came to a decision. Of all of them, Granville seemed the most levelheaded. "You've treated me decent, so I have to be honest with you. I haven't told you the whole truth."

"About what?"

"I was on a scout for the army when I ran into you. I'm with a patrol out of Fort Laramie."

"What in tarnation is a patrol doin' way up here?"

"Looking for some homesteaders they've heard about who have settled somewhere near Flathead Lake."

"The hell you say. Why would the army be lookin' for us?"

"To ask you to leave."

Granville drew sharp rein. "What gives them any say in where we've set down our roots?"

"They thought you might have settled on Flathead land. The government has a treaty with the Flatheads and doesn't want to see it broken."

"Lord Almighty. And you didn't tell me this until now?" Granville clucked to his sorrel. "What a thing to drop on a man."

"If it helps any, I don't think you are on Flathead land," Fargo said. "Based on what I know of the treaty, you're right outside the reservation, not on it."

"How sure are you of that?"

"The south end of Flathead Lake isn't part of the reservation, and you're near the south end."

"Hold on. The government set up a reservation for these Flat-headers, you say?"

"They did."

"And the lake is part of the reservation?"

"It is."

"But only part of the lake?"

Fargo nodded.

Granville looked confused. "What sense is there to givin' the Injuns part of the lake and not the whole thing?"

"You'd have to ask the government."

"Those in office don't have much common sense. There have been times when I'd swear they complicate things on purpose." Granville cocked his head. "But back to this patrol. Do they know where me and mine are?"

"Not yet. I haven't told them."

"Are you goin' to?"

"I'm supposed to."

"Well, hell."

They rode in silence until they neared the next clearing and the next cabin.

"That's Vernon's," Granville said. "Do me a favor and don't mention any of this patrol business to him or any of the others. Some have tempers and might not take it kindly."

"I won't say a word to anyone until you say otherwise," Fargo assured him.

"I'm obliged. I need to ponder on it some before I bring it up." Granville gazed out across the valley. "We like it here. It would upset everybody no end if the government asked us to leave."

Just then a small child let out a whoop. Kids poured from everywhere to greet Uncle Granville and jabber. Vernon introduced his wife, and after Granville politely declined an invite to tea, they were under way again.

"You can see how it is?" Granville immediately took up their talk again. "You can see how happy everyone is?"

"I can," Fargo said.

"This here is paradise. There's plenty of game, and the Injuns leave us be." Granville bobbed his head at the clear blue vault of sky. "Doesn't rain much, though. It's been weeks since we saw a drop. The woods are tinder dry."

"Summers are usually that way," Fargo said. "You get a few

thunderstorms, but the heavy rains don't start until the fall. After that, the snows come."

"Are the winters really as bad as you made them out to be?"

"Sometimes they're worse," Fargo said. "The blizzards can come on you out of nowhere. If you're caught in the woods, you lose all sense of direction. And it can become so cold you'll freeze without a fire."

"That sounds like experience talkin'."

"It is."

"Damn. We'll have to lay up enough firewood to last months. We'll have to stock up on jerked venison and the like, too."

The next cabin was Solomon's, where they were greeted just as warmly. After that, it was Rufus's homestead. Rufus's wife was a walking tent with a face as wide as the moon and the disposition of a riled she-bear.

"That woman scares me sometimes," Granville admitted as they rode off. "Remember Rufus sayin' she doesn't boss him around? Why, he can't hardly breathe without her say-so."

"True love," Fargo said.

Granville laughed.

Eventually they rounded a bend and the last clearing appeared.

"That there is Lester's," Granville said.

No sooner were the words out of his mouth than a shot rang out.

# 13

Fargo heard the buzz of lead over their heads. He went to rein toward cover but stopped when Granville gave a holler.

"Who's doin' that shootin? It's Granville, consarn you! What are you shootin' at us for?"

Only then did Fargo realize the clearing was empty. There were no kids anywhere, as there had been at all the others. The cabin door was shut, and a rifle barrel was poking past burlap that covered a window.

"Lester, you hear me in there?"

A man's voice was raised in anger, and there was a loud squawk. The rifle barrel was jerked back, and in a few moments, the front door was flung wide and out hobbled a man using a crutch fashioned from a tree limb. He was holding the rifle in his other hand and waved it at them.

"It's all right, Granville. It was Beaumont doin' the shootin'. He took you for the outlaws."

"Beaumont?" Granville said to himself. "Why, the boy ain't hardly old enough to hold a gun, let alone shoot one."

Out of the cabin filed the rest of Lester's family. All eleven of them. Lester was the skinniest of all the men. His wife weighed about an ounce more. Of their children, six were girls. The eldest was the same age as Darlene, and nearly as pretty, only her hair was black. Lester and his wife had named her Periwinkle.

The boy who'd fired the rifle was the youngest, and barely taller than the rifle he'd used.

"Say you're sorry, Beaumont," Lester demanded. "You could have taken Uncle Granville's head off."

"Or mine," Fargo said.

Beaumont had his hands clasped in front of him, and his head was bowed as if he regretted what he'd done, but there was a defiant cast to his jaw and his eyes. "It's his fault," he said, pointing at Fargo.

"How so?" Lester said.

"He's not one of us. I took him for an outlaw."

"Who happened to be ridin' with your uncle and payin' us a visit?"

"He could have made Uncle Granville bring him," Beaumont said sulkily. "It could've been a trick."

"From now on, don't go shootin' at people unless you get my say-so first," Lester said. "Me, or your ma's. You're too young to be killin' yet, anyway. Another year or so, then you can."

"I won't let anyone hurt us," Beaumont said. "You gettin' hurt was enough."

Lester was touched. "We just have to be careful when it comes to shootin' folks. You shoot the wrong one and it can bother you some."

"Wouldn't bother me," Beaumont said.

Lester handed the rifle to him. "Take this back inside, would you?"

Relieved that he wasn't being punished, the boy dashed indoors.

All this time the other children had been eyeing Fargo with curiosity. All except Periwinkle.

Fargo flattered himself that she was eyeing him for a whole different reason. When he smiled, her cheeks turned pink, and she shyly looked away. He almost got hard, right there.

"Now, then," Lester said to Granville. "Who is this fella and why have you brought him?"

"He's a scout," Granville replied. "He was set on by the same bunch that set on you, and he's trackin' them down. He'd like to hear what happened. It might help him some."

Lester nodded. "Fine by me. The missus will put coffee on and we can jaw a spell." He glanced at her and she smiled and nodded and went in. "Now, then," he said again. Apparently it was a pet phrase of his. "How about I show you?" He started around to the side of the cabin.

The kids trailed after them. Periwinkle hung back, but she never took her eyes off Fargo.

Like the rest of the homesteads, this one had a large corral. They needed it. There was a horse for every member of the family, plus pack mules.

"It must take a lot to keep all of them fed," Fargo remarked.

Lester pointed at a huge pile of grass to one side. "There's a meadow not far from here. We get a lot from there, and from near the lake. It keeps the young'uns busy totin' it, but the work is good for them. Chores build character." He gave his offspring a loving look.

The kids didn't seem nearly as happy about it.

"There's a small stream nearby where we take the critters to drink," Lester related. "I also dug a well but haven't put in a pump yet, so we have to haul the water up in a bucket. Takes forever."

"About the outlaws?" Fargo prompted.

"Oh. It was late, pushin' ten or so, and I was about to turn in. My missus and the kids were all asleep. I heard a ruckus. The horses were actin' up, so I taken my rifle and came out to see if a panther or a bear was nosin' around."

"Tell him the mistake you made," Granville said.

"I brought a lantern with me," Lester said sheepishly. "But how was I to know it was men and not a bear or a cat?"

"Go on," Granville said.

"Well, I walked up to the corral and the horses were all starin' into the woods yonder, so I stared, too, and that's when one of the varmints shot at me." Lester tapped a finger to a furrow on the

42

top rail. "See this? I reckon he was aimin' at my head, but it hit here and got deflected into my leg."

"You were lucky," Granville said.

"The Good Lord was lookin' out for me, that's for sure," Lester said.

"What happened after you were shot?" Fargo asked.

"I fell down. What do you think happened?"

"Did more of them shoot at you? Did they come after you? How did you get back inside?"

"Oh. No, some of them started to come out of the woods. I could see 'em but not too clearly. I took a few shots and they took a few more, but no one hit anybody. Then my family came runnin' out, and my oldest girls and boys can shoot, and they cut loose and the polecats skedaddled."

Fargo couldn't see Latham and his killers running from kids. Then again, the oldest were between fifteen and twenty, and with half a dozen of the family shooting back, Latham might have decided it wasn't worth the risk.

"Wasn't much to it, actually," Lester was saying. "Sort of silly when you think about it. Outlaws out to rob *us*? We're about as poor as can be."

"Maybe they were after somethin' other than money," Granville said.

"I don't see what," Lester said.

Fargo did. He was staring at Periwinkle.

## 14

Fargo had a choice to make. He could accept Lester's invite to stay for supper, or he could go back with Granville and have supper at his place. That wasn't what he had to make up his mind about, though. The real choice was between Darlene and Periwinkle.

Fargo could tell Periwinkle was interested. Darlene had been, too. But which was mostly likely to give him a tumble was the big question. Darlene had been more open, if discreet. But shy ones like Periwinkle were often bundles of surprises. *Which to pick? Which to pick?* he asked himself.

Everyone was standing around outside and Granville had just remarked that he should be getting home when young Beaumont piped up with "But what if those bad men come back, Uncle? You should stick around."

"They could strike at any of us, son," Lester said.

"But they know you're hurt, Pa," Beaumont said. "They might figure we'd be easier pickin's."

Fargo agreed. "Tell you what," he said. "I'll stay the night, just in case. Outside, where I won't be any bother and can keep an eye on things."

"That's awful kind of you," the wife said.

"Yes," Periwinkle said, "it is."

Lester thoughtfully rubbed his chin, and nodded. "I won't deny it'd help to make me rest a little easier knowin' you're here to help. But it shouldn't all be on you. I'll stay outside, too."

Fargo would rather Lester didn't. Periwinkle wasn't about to pay him a nocturnal visit with her father outside.

Lester's wife unwittingly came to his aid. "I'd rather you stayed inside with us. You hardly got a lick of sleep last night and you're still weak from the blood you lost."

"It's not right Fargo does it himself," Lester insisted.

"Listen to your missus," Fargo said. "You won't be of any use if you can't keep your eyes open. Send someone out to check on me now and then if that will make you feel better."

"I'll do the checkin', Pa," Periwinkle volunteered. "I can be as sneaky as a man when I put my mind to it."

"Yes, girl, you can," Lester conceded. "But you could end up shot like me."

"Let her do it," the mother said. "You need your rest."

"Yes, Priscilla, dear," Lester said.

Granville glanced at Fargo and grinned and winked. "Rufus and him have a lot in common, don't they?"

"What's that about Rufus?" Priscilla asked.

"Oh, it was nothin'," Granville replied, and swung onto his sorrel. "You folks be careful, you hear? Whoever these outlaws are, I've got a feelin' we haven't seen the last of them." With a smile and a wave, Granville reined around and headed down the valley. The woods swallowed him, but they heard him whistling for a while.

The family didn't say a word until the whistling faded. Fargo could tell they were apprehensive over the outlaws. He didn't blame them.

"Now, then," Lester said with a cough. "It'll be hours yet till night falls. Why don't you come in and sit awhile?"

"I'd like to scout around," Fargo said.

"I'll go with you, mister," Beaumont said. "I can show you some of their tracks."

"I don't know," the mother said.

Periwinkle stepped forward and placed a hand on her little brother's shoulder. "I'll go with them, Ma, and keep an eye on Beaumont."

"All right." Priscilla jabbed a finger at Fargo. "But don't you let anything happen to them, you hear?"

Without being obvious, Fargo ran his gaze from Periwinkle's smooth neck to her ankles. "Don't worry, ma'am. I want to keep them in one piece as much as you do."

Moving to the Ovaro, he slid the Henry from the saddle scabbard.

"Why, lookee there," Lester exclaimed. "That's about the shiniest rifle I ever did see. A Henry, ain't it?"

"It is," Fargo confirmed.

"I've heard about them, but I've never seen one. Is it true you can load one on Sunday and shoot it all week?"

"If you don't shoot more than sixteen times." Fargo set him straight. That was how many the Henry held, fully loaded: fifteen in the tubular magazine and another cartridge in the chamber.

"I'd like to get me one someday, but they cost a pretty penny," Lester lamented.

Fargo started around the corral.

Beaumont and Periwinkle came up on the other side, Periwinkle smiling bashfully.

A hush lay over the forest. The afternoon was waning, and dark patches of shadow alternated with sparkling sunbeams that pierced the forest canopy like shimmering swords. A lot of the pines were turning brown from the lack of rain.

The oaks showed less strain, although if the rains didn't come on time, their leaves, too, would brown and shrivel.

Fargo reached out with his senses but detected nothing out of the ordinary. Not that he expected the outlaws to be skulking about in broad daylight. Latham would wait for the cover of dark.

"Want me to show you the tracks I found?" young Beaumont asked eagerly.

Fargo motioned. "After you."

The boy scampered to the task, threading through the trees with the alacrity of youth.

"Not so fast, boy," Fargo said. "There's no hurry." Not when he wanted to spend time with Periwinkle.

"He's tryin' to impress you." She spoke to him directly for the first time. "I suspect he's taken a shine to you. What with your fancy rifle and those buckskins and all."

"How about you?" Fargo asked. "Have you taken a shine to me, too?"

Her cheeks turned pinker than before. "It's not proper for a lady to take a shine to a man she hardly knows."

"I've taken a shine to you."

"You have?" Periwinkle said, sounding delighted but trying to hide the fact.

Fargo cut straight to the chase. "I was hoping we could spend some time together tonight."

"You were?" Periwinkle said, and blinked. "Goodness. You're not one for beatin' around the bush, are you?"

"Not when it comes to that," Fargo admitted.

"I don't know," Periwinkle said. "My ma would kill me if she caught us."

Fargo inwardly grinned. She hadn't come right out and said no. "Think it over. I'm just letting you know I'm interested. If you're not, that's fine."

"I never said I wasn't," Periwinkle said quickly, and caught herself. "That is, sure, I'll ruminate on it some."

"Ruminate?" Fargo said, and laughed.

"It's a word I picked up from my uncle Solomon. He uses big ones from time to time. Comes from him bein' the only one of us who can read." Periwinkle smiled self-consciously. "I like to use 'em 'cause it makes me sound smart. 'Ruminate' is one of my favorites."

Fargo took a gamble. "I have a favorite word."

"You do? Let me hear it."

Bending, Fargo whispered in her ear.

Periwinkle gasped and nearly turned purple, but she didn't smack him. Instead she giggled and said, "I can tell you're goin' to be a handful."

"You, too," Fargo said, looking at her breasts.

46

# 15

The boot prints were in soft earth along the stream Lester had mentioned. It was a ribbon of water, hardly inches deep in spots. Not one but two sets of prints showed where a couple of the outlaws had stood awhile, probably right before they closed in on the cabin.

"I found them my own self," Beaumont declared proudly.

"You'll make a fine tracker if you keep at it," Fargo encouraged him. "See if you can find some more."

The boy dashed off, following the stream.

"Did you do that on purpose?" Periwinkle asked. "So you and me could be alone?"

Fargo stepped close enough that his chest practically brushed her breasts. "What do you think?"

"Oh my." Periwinkle half turned away as if embarrassed, but she glanced at him, down low. "I thought you wanted to wait until tonight."

"Do you?" Fargo asked, and ran his hand along her forearm.

Periwinkle was like her pa and had a favorite saying. "Oh my," she said again. "That felt nice."

"How about this?" Fargo looped his arm around her waist and pulled her to him. She didn't resist. When he bent his mouth to hers, she timidly pressed into him. He let the kiss linger awhile, and when he pulled back, she was breathing heavily. "Liked that, did you?"

Periwinkle nodded, and wouldn't meet his eyes.

"Something the matter?"

"I shouldn't be doin' this," she said, "and yet I want to so much."

Fargo was about to kiss her again when a holler from out of the undergrowth intruded.

"Mr. Fargo!" Beaumont bawled. "Over here! Look at what I found!"

"Damn," Fargo said, unwinding his arm.

Grinning, Periwinkle said, "That's my little brother for you. He always picks the worst time to do things. My sisters or me will be as busy as can be and he'll need somethin' done."

"Mr. Fargo! Mr. Fargo!"

"If we don't go," Periwinkle said, "he'll keep yellin' from now until doomsday. He has lungs on him like you wouldn't believe."

"Wonderful," Fargo said.

Periwinkle laughed.

Fargo figured the boy had come across more tracks. He came around a bend and saw Beaumont with a long stick in his hand, poking at something in a small pine.

"What did he do?" Periwinkle wondered. "Catch a poor squirrel with its guard down?"

Fargo doubted it. A squirrel could easily leap from the small pine to another tree and escape. He took a couple more steps and drew up short. "Son of a bitch," he blurted.

"Oh Lordy," Periwinkle said.

A black bear cub, so young it had to be fresh out of the den, was clinging to the pine with all four paws. Terrified by the boy's antics, it threw back its head and bawled.

"Beaumont, no!" Periwinkle cried, and ran toward him.

Beaumont was having a grand time. He poked at the cub's quivering leg and cackled.

Fargo would have thought that a backwoodsman like Lester would have taught his son better. "Boy, cut it out!" he shouted.

Beaumont stopped poking and looked over his shoulder just as Periwinkle reached him and smacked him on the shoulder. "Hey!"

"What do you think you're doin'? What have Pa and Ma said about bears? Are you tryin' to get torn to ribbons?"

"It's just a cub," Beaumont protested. "I saw it, and it ran up this little tree. I was teasin' it, is all."

"You blamed nuisance," Periwinkle scolded. "You're lucky the mother bear ain't anywhere around."

The underbrush crackled and crashed, and out of it hurtled two hundred and fifty pounds of furious she-bear. Head low, ears back, she roared and advanced on Periwinkle and her brother, who were rooted in shock.

Fargo didn't want to shoot the mother. She was only protecting her cub.

Snapping the Henry to his shoulder, he fired into the ground in front of her. At the blast the mother bear halted. "Back away from her," he told Periwinkle and Beaumont, "nice and slow."

Periwinkle began to, but her brother just stood there. Gripping his wrist, she pulled him after her.

Beaumont shook the stick at the mother bear and hollered, "You come any closer and I'll swat you."

"Drop the damn stick," Fargo snapped.

When Beaumont didn't, Periwinkle tore it from his grasp and threw it to one side. They reached Fargo and he said for them to keep going while he backed after them, covering the bear.

When they had gone far enough that she didn't deem them a threat, the mother bear quickly moved to the small pine and nosed her offspring. The cub wasted no time in clambering down. A few moments more, and mother and the little one had moved off into the undergrowth.

Fargo let out a breath and lowered his Henry. "That was a stupid stunt, boy. You could have gotten yourself killed."

"I was just playing," Beaumont said.

"We're going back," Fargo informed them. Their family would have heard the shot and be worried. "Beaumont, run ahead and let them know we're all fine."

"Why me?" the boy wanted to know.

"Because you were the idiot who provoked the bear. Now go." Fargo could hear shouts from the vicinity of the cabin.

The boy grumbled, but did.

Cradling the Henry, Fargo gave a last glance back to be sure the black bear was gone.

"You were wonderful," Periwinkle said.

"All I did was shoot into the ground."

"You saved us," Periwinkle insisted. "If you hadn't been there, that bear might have torn us apart."

Fargo let her think what she wanted. Black bears rarely killed people.

Periwinkle was gazing at him dreamily. "I don't know how I can ever thank you," she said softly.

Grinning and winking, Fargo said, "I do. Tonight when we're alone."

As usual, she blushed. But she didn't say no.

# 16

Supper was an experience.

Lester's wife went to extra effort because of Fargo. They had roast elk garnished with wild onions, potatoes dripping with butter, and small wheat cakes she whipped up and smeared with jam.

"Why, will you look at this?" Lester marveled when the dishes and bowls had been set out in the middle of the table. "My missus has outdone herself. We haven't had a feed like this in a coon's age."

"There was no need to go to all this trouble on my account, ma'am," Fargo said, although he was mightily pleased. He rarely got to eat home cooking.

"It was nothin'," Priscilla said in a way that suggested she knew perfectly well it was special.

The kids were well mannered at the table. They didn't yammer or fight over food; they were too busy stuffing their mouths. Watching them, Fargo was reminded of a starving pack of wolves he once saw tear into a moose the pack had brought down.

The only one not in a good mood was Beaumont. For his "harebrained bear stunt," as Lester called it, he was to perform extra chores for a week.

"I hate chores," the boy had declared when his father announced the punishment.

"Maybe next time you'll think twice before you go pokin' some cub," Lester had said.

"I didn't hurt it or nothin'."

"That's enough sass out of you, boy," the mother had interjected. "You're lucky we don't take a switch to your backside."

About halfway through the meal, Lester chuckled and said with his mouth full of potatoes, "Can my missus cook or can she cook?"

Fargo glanced at Periwinkle's chest and forked a piece of venison into his mouth. "You have a fine family."

Lester nodded and beamed. "Yes, sir, the Good Lord has blessed us. I hope he keeps on blessin' us. I don't mind admittin' these outlaws have me worried. Why pick on poor folk like us?"

"You have horses. You have guns." Fargo paused, debating whether to say it. "You have women."

The older daughters all looked at him.

"Yes, well," Lester said. "Men like that are vermin. They should be staked out and skinned."

"Lester," the wife said. "Not at the table."

"Well, they should."

Fargo ate until he was fit to burst. Afterward, while Priscilla and the children did the dishes, he and Lester sat at the table, drinking coffee.

Lester produced a pipe. "So, tell me," he said as he got out his tobacco, "what do you reckon the chances are that those polecats will come back? You say you ran into them. Did you get the idea they're plannin' to leave this neck of the country?"

"No."

"Well, damn."

"If we make it hard for them, they'll light a shuck," Fargo predicted. "Outlaws don't like it when their victims put up too much of a fight."

"I hope you're right. The last thing we need is that kind of trouble."

Several of the younger ones had already turned in when Fargo rose and excused himself. "I'll be out by the corral," he let them know. For two reasons. First, the horses would alert him if anyone came near. Second, and more important, he could keep an eye on the Ovaro.

"Do you want to take a lantern with you?" the wife asked.

"No, ma'am," Fargo said. He almost added, "And be shot at like your husband was?"

The night was crystal clear, as only the nights in the mountains could be. A host of stars twinkled. Pale light, courtesy of a crescent moon, bathed the corral and the forest.

Somewhere in the woods an owl hooted, and in the distance a coyote wailed a lonesome lament.

Fargo sat with his back to the rails and his Henry across his lap. He wasn't tired. The prospect of being attacked by Latham's bunch had something to do with it. The prospect of dallying with Periwinkle had even more.

An hour dragged, then two. He was about convinced she had

changed her mind when he heard the cabin door quietly open and the soft pad of steps as she came around the corral.

"There you are," she whispered, and sank down.

"Are they all asleep?"

"No. Ma and Pa are still up. Which is why I can't stay. I'll be back later, once they've turned in. I promise." Periwinkle smiled and went to go.

"What's your hurry?" Fargo asked, putting his hand on her arm. "You can spend a few minutes, can't you?"

"What do you want to talk about?"

"Who said anything about talking?" Fargo replied, and pulled her against him. She surprised him by taking his chin in her hands and trying to suck his tongue down her throat. When they broke apart, her eyes were limpid pools of need.

"That was awful nice," she said.

"There's more where it came from."

"You have me wantin' you so much I can't think straight. It's all I've thought about all evenin'."

"Good."

"Have you thought about me?"

"With every breath." Fargo laid it on a bit thick.

"Lordy," Periwinkle said, resting her forehead on his chin. "I wasn't fixin' to get married for a while yet."

"What?"

"You and me," Periwinkle said, gazing into his eyes. "It's all so suddenlike. I asked Ma, and she said that's how it was with her, too. She took one look at my pa and she knew."

"Wait," Fargo said. "You've talked to your mother about me?"

"Of course, silly goose." Periwinkle pecked him on the cheek. "A girl tells her ma everything. Didn't you know that? Especially when it comes to the man she's fixin' to marry." She smiled and turned and scooted off.

"Well, hell," Fargo said.

# 17

Fargo was annoyed with himself. He was so used to saloon doves falling over him that he tended to forget girls like Periwinkle, raised in a God-fearing family, didn't throw themselves at every gent who came down the road. Here he'd been dropping hints about the two of them making love and she thought he was dropping hints about the two of them spending the rest of their days together.

"Damn me, anyway," he grumbled.

There were three things in life he loved. Three things he sometimes found it hard to go without. Foremost was his wanderlust, his craving to see what lay over the next horizon. Next was his fondness for whiskey and cards. Third was his hankering for the ladies. Tall ones, short ones, city girl or country gal, blond, brunette, redhead—he didn't care. They were the apples in the pie of life, and he enjoyed nothing so much as taking a juicy bite out of them.

Not Periwinkle, though. Not now. He wasn't like some men who promised women anything to get up their skirts. He had to think of a way to let her down easy.

The snap of a twig in the woods put an end to his reflection. He listened for a while but heard nothing else to suggest the outlaws had returned. And the horses in the corral were all dozing.

Settling back, Fargo moved the Henry from his lap and propped it against a rail and yawned. The long day and his last meal were catching up to him.

Fargo imagined that Captain Benson would be wondering where he got to. By now the patrol would have moved on around Flathead Lake and probably be camped along the shore. He needed to report back. But once he did, it might cause trouble for the Tennesseans.

Fargo liked these people. They were down-to-earth, friendly folk who only wanted to be left alone to live where and as they pleased. They were no threat to anyone and would get along fine with the Flatheads, who were friendly to whites who were friendly to them.

The Ovaro picked that moment to raise its head and prick its ears.

Instantly alert, Fargo grabbed the Henry. Anything could be out there. A mountain lion. That she-bear and her cub.

A second and third horse did the same as his stallion. All three stared into the forest to the north.

Fargo flattened and crawled to where he could see the tree line. It could be that Latham figured the homesteaders wouldn't expect him to return so soon, and must figure they were asleep by now.

But as the minutes dragged and no one appeared, Fargo decided he must be mistaken. It had been an animal and nothing more.

Then several shadows separated from tree trunks and stalked into the clearing in a crouch.

Fargo recollected there were seven, all told. The other four might be converging from different directions.

Fixing a bead on one of those approaching the corral, he thumbed back the Henry's hammer.

Just then the hinges on the front door squeaked. Someone was coming out of the cabin.

The three shadows went prone.

Fargo swore under his breath. He didn't have a good shot at any of them. Even more worrisome, whoever came out of the cabin was oblivious of the peril. Three guesses who, he told himself.

"Skye?" Periwinkle whispered. "Where are you?"

One of the outlaws heaved up and dashed toward the corral. The moonlight played over a cruel countenance crowned by a beaver hat. It was the one called Hagler.

Fargo shot him. He didn't shout a warning or demand the outlaw throw down his guns. He centered a bead and stroked the trigger.

Hagler was spun half around, cried out, and fell. At his outcry, the two men on the ground and others in the woods cut loose.

Fargo hugged the dirt. They were shooting at his muzzle flash, and slugs hit on both sides of him and in front of his face.

Hagler rose and stumbled toward the woods. His two pards rushed to help, one fanning shots in Fargo's direction. Fargo couldn't get off another shot until they were almost to the trees.

He rose and fired and had to flatten again as leaden hail pock-marked the ground around him. He saw the muzzle flashes of two shooters in the woods. Counting Hagler and his companions, that accounted for five of the seven outlaws. He wondered where the last two had gotten to.

Hagler made it to cover. A few more shots were fired, someone shouted, and the shooting stopped.

Fargo quickly reloaded. Afraid that the two who were unaccounted for might have circled around the clearing, he turned and crawled along the corral fence. He hadn't gone far when he stopped and stiffened.

A body lay sprawled near where he had been sitting earlier.

He scrambled over.

Periwinkle lay on her side, her hair over her face. She had a hand splayed to her side but was so limp that for a few heartbeats Fargo feared she was dead. Then she groaned and rolled onto her back.

"I'm shot."

Kneeling, Fargo said gruffly, "I can see that." He moved her hand and practically had to stick his nose in her wound to tell how serious it was.

"I don't want to die," Periwinkle said, and sniffled.

"It's a scratch," Fargo informed her. "You were nicked, is all. Unless it becomes infected, you'll be fine."

"Oh, thank you," Periwinkle said, and threw her arms around him in gratitude, as if he had something to do with her only suffering a graze.

Fargo slid his arms under her.

"What are you doin'?"

"Carrying you." Fargo lifted her and hastened to the front door. He only had to kick it once and the door was flung wide by Beaumont.

"Pa! Ma! Come quick. Sis has blood on her."

The family had thrown on clothes and grabbed their artillery and were about to rush out to help.

Priscilla had Fargo deposit Periwinkle on her blankets. They didn't have beds. The cabin was too small. There was a bedroom for the parents and a bedroom the children had to share.

Fargo stepped back out, and the family swarmed her in concern. Since he'd only be in the way, he went to a side window that gave a partial view of the corral. The horses had calmed down; the night was still.

Lester hobbled over. "Are they still out there?"

"Don't appear to be."

"How'd she get hit?"

"Stray bullet."

"If'n I've told them once, I've told them a thousand times to hunt cover when lead starts to fly."

"If you'll keep watch here, I'll go see if they're still out there."

"It shouldn't be on your shoulders," Lester said. "This is my homestead."

"How quiet can you be with one good leg?"

"Not very."

Fargo moved aside so Lester could stand at the window. "You see anyone who isn't me, shoot him."

"It might be hard to tell in the dark. I wouldn't want to hit you by mistake."

"On second thought," Fargo said, "let me do the shooting." Slipping outside, he went around to the opposite side. The woods were quiet. Just when he was convinced it was safe and took a step into the open, someone coughed.

## 18

Fargo darted back, hoping he hadn't been spotted. He glimpsed a silhouette amid the spruce; it was there and it was gone. Shortly thereafter he thought he heard the faint jingle of a spur.

More time went by, and nothing happened.

Fargo was tired of waiting. He burst toward the forest in a zigzag. Once in the trees, he squatted.

Not so much as a cricket chirped.

The carpet of needles underfoot muffled his tread. He'd gone a short way when he pricked his ears. Voices had carried on the breeze, too far off to make sense of the words.

Fargo made for them. Presently he spied movement, and a

horse nickered. Throwing caution aside, he broke into a run. He wanted to drop as many as he could before they got away, but it wasn't to be.

Emerging into a small clearing where the outlaws had left their mounts when they attacked the cabin, he was just in time to see a cluster of riders fade into the night. He jerked his rifle up but lowered it again. "Damn."

Disappointed, Fargo headed back. Holding the Henry in his left hand, he rested the barrel on his shoulder.

It hadn't occurred to him that the outlaws might have left one of their number to keep an eye on Lester's. Or that the gunman might decide to kill him quietlike so as not to alert Lester's family.

His blunder was borne home when a man sprang from concealment and thrust a knife at his neck. By purest chance, the Henry's barrel deflected the blade, but the blow knocked the rifle from Fargo's hand. He clawed for his Colt, but the outlaw stabbed at his chest. Instinctively he grabbed the outlaw's wrist while at the same instant the man seized his to keep him from drawing the Colt.

Dappled by moon-tossed shadows, they grappled. The man tried to trip Fargo, but Fargo hopped over his leg. In return, Fargo rammed a knee at the man's groin, but the outlaw took it on his hip.

The man kicked at Fargo's knee. Fargo sidestepped, twisted, and hooked a boot behind the outlaw's leg. He pushed, thinking to topple him, but the man shifted somehow and slipped free.

Fargo strained to unlimber his Colt. One shot and it would be over.

The outlaw suddenly wrenched free of Fargo's grip, let go of Fargo's wrist, and flew toward a thicket, drawing his six-shooter as he went.

Fargo did some flying of his own. He made it behind a pine just as the man's six-gun boomed. He aimed at the thicket, but there was no one to shoot. Darting to another tree, he crouched and waited for the outlaw to give himself away. He heard nothing, saw nothing. After their flurry of violence, the woods had gone quiet again.

Dropping onto his belly, Fargo crawled to a different tree. He straightened to his full height and peered over a low branch. The thicket and the adjacent woods were empty of movement.

Wondering where the man could have gotten to, Fargo received his answer when boots drummed. That was followed by the sound of hooves rapidly receding into the night.

Fargo swore. It just wasn't his night.

Voices from the cabin spurred him into hurrying back. Everyone was up and armed for war. Even Periwinkle.

Fargo explained about his clash, and that the last of the outlaws was gone. "You're safe for the rest of the night, at least."

"I hope to God you're right," Lester said. "All this shootin' is frayin' on our nerves." He and his wife commenced to shoo the young ones back to their blankets.

Periwinkle came over. "I'm sorry," she whispered so no one else would hear. "I won't be able to sneak out later."

"Didn't expect you would," Fargo said.

She touched his hand. "I want you to know I'm still interested, though. I've thought about it and thought about it, and you would make any woman as fine a husband as there is."

Fargo needed a drink. He asked Lester about it after everyone else had turned in.

Lester glanced at the door to the bedroom he and his wife shared. "I could use a nip my own self. My missus doesn't approve, though. Priscilla ain't a drinkin' gal. But she does allow as how it's good for a man's constitution now and then. And if this ain't one of those times, I don't know when is." He indicated Fargo should take a seat at the table while he hobbled to the cupboard, stretched onto his toes to reach the top shelf, moved a few glasses aside, and returned with a half-empty bottle of Monongahela. "Will this do?"

"Right as rain," Fargo said.

Lester returned with two glasses, poured until each was half-full, and raised his. "To killin' every one of those sons of bitches."

Fargo grunted, touched his glass to Lester's, and swallowed gratefully. It more than hit the spot.

"I want to thank you for all your help," Lester said. "If you weren't here, I might have been dead by now."

"Your family is pretty tough."

"That they are," Lester said proudly. "But tough doesn't always beat mean, and those outlaws are as snake-mean as they come. They'd have to be, to want to harm a woman and her children."

"Men like them," Fargo said, "are why guns were invented."

Lester chuckled. "They do deserve killin', if anybody ever did."

"I'm surprised none of your kin haven't come to help," Fargo mentioned. He would have thought that Solomon, at least, would have heard the shots. His homestead was nearest.

"All of them turn in early. You ever hear the sayin' that early to bed and early to rise make a fella healthy and wise?"

"I've heard something like that," Fargo said.

"Our family has always been early bedders and early risers, but to tell you the truth, it ain't made any of us all that wise."

"You're not doing bad. You have a good cabin, a good family."

"True, true," Lester conceded, taking another swallow. "I sort of envy you, though, bein' so footloose and fancy-free. You don't have a passel of loved ones to provide for and worry about."

"That's a bad thing?"

"No, not at all," Lester backtracked. He gazed sorrowfully at the bedroom doors. "I just don't want anything to happen to them."

"We won't let it."

Lester smiled. "I never would have taken you for carin' much about others, but I reckon you do." He drained his glass, stood, and brought the bottle back to the cupboard.

"I'd better get to bed. This leg is botherin' me and I'm powerful tired." He used his crutch and took a step and looked back. "I almost forgot. My missus says that Periwinkle has set her sights on you."

"About that," Fargo said, but got no further.

"It's all right if you're interested in her," Lester said. "Priscilla and me think you'll be a fine addition to the family." He smiled and nodded. "Well, good night, friend. Or should I call you my son-in-law?" He entered the bedroom.

Fargo sighed and summed up his feelings with "This pecker of mine gets me in more trouble than I know what to do with."

# 19

The squawk of a jay woke Fargo at the first blush of light to the east. He'd fallen asleep sitting with his back to a corral post and the Henry across his legs. Sitting up, he stretched and yawned.

Not a sound came from the cabin, but it wouldn't stay that way for long.

Rising, Fargo walked around the corral to get his blood flowing. He needed to make up his mind how much longer he was going to stay. Captain Benson would be expecting him to report back.

The stars faded as the blue of dawn slowly spread from east to west. The sliver of moon relinquished its reign.

A few dark clouds had drifted in to the northwest. Not enough to constitute a storm front, but they would bearing watching.

As Fargo came around the cabin, the front door opened and out hobbled Lester.

"Mornin', son-in-law."

"About that," Fargo said again.

Lester grinned and held up his hand. "No need to say a word. That's between you and her. If it works out, fine and dandy. If not, fine and dandy, too." He paused. "So long as you don't take advantage, I'll keep my nose out of it."

Fargo was about to say that he'd be heading out in a bit, but Lester's wife picked that moment to holler, "Lester, let him know I'll have vittles ready in two shakes of a lamb's tail. We've got some eggs left and that ham we might as well use up. I have coffee on, too, if he likes some in the mornin'."

"You heard her," Lester said. "You're welcome to join us."

Fargo wasn't about to pass up another chance at a home-cooked meal. He leaned against the wall and waited as the kids scampered about tending to the horses and other chores.

Periwinkle emerged. She had on a different dress, probably her best, and had brushed her hair. "Mornin'. Did you get much sleep?"

"Enough," Fargo said.

She looked both ways, then whispered, "I dreamed of you. Of you and me—" She stopped and blushed.

"About that," Fargo said, and realized he had a new favorite expression of his own.

Periwinkle placed her hand on his arm. "I talked to my ma, and she's worried that we might be rushin' things. She said maybe we should take it slow, that it's better if there's courtin' before the I-dos."

"She's a smart woman," Fargo said, grasping at the straw.

"What I'm sayin' is," Periwinkle went on, "that if you'd like to court me, you're welcome to. Then after six months or a year, you can get down on bended knee so it's done proper." She grinned and kissed him on the cheek and went back inside.

"I *really* need a drink," Fargo said. He didn't realize anyone else was there until a small voice piped up.

"Want me to fetch you some water?"

Fargo looked down. "What are you up to?"

Beaumont's thumbs were hooked in his suspenders, and he was chewing on a blade of grass. "Nothin' much. Heard as how you're goin' to be part of the family and reckoned I should get to know you better."

"Oh hell."

"Ma and Pa were talkin' about how after you and sis are hitched, everybody will pitch in and help you clear land and build your own cabin. Ma was thinkin' it should be just a little ways away, so she can come visit a lot."

Fargo bit off a string of choice swearwords. This was getting out of hand. He considered leaving without eating, but his stomach cast its vote by growling.

"Ma says I should thank you for not lettin' that black bear hurt us yesterday. She said what I did was pretty stupid."

"There's a lot of that going around."

"Well, I'm just sayin', if you do end up bein' my uncle, I'll try not to get bears mad at us."

"This family is a wonderment," Fargo said.

"After you're hitched to my sis, can I ride your horse?"

"No."

"Why not? We'd be kin, and Pa always says that kin should always be nice to other kin."

"No one rides my horse but me."

"That's awful selfish."

"Don't you have chores to do?"

"I'm done those that need doin' before breakfast. How about if we ride him together? I've ridden double with Pa before. You have a bigger behind than he does, but we'd both fit on your saddle."

"Someone shoot me," Fargo said.

"Why would you say a silly thing like that? Bein' shot ain't fun. Just ask my pa and my sister."

"Damn it all." Fargo rolled his eyes skyward and saw there were more dark clouds than before.

"You cuss a lot," Beaumont remarked. "Once you're hitched, that won't do. Ma doesn't like cussin'. Pa does it now and then, and she about boxes his ears. You'll have to learn to stop or she's liable to box yours."

Fargo turned and looked in the window in the hope the family was about to sit down to eat. Two of the girls were setting the table.

"Yes, sir," Beaumont said. "I'd like to ride your horse and I'd like to shoot that rifle of yours. Pa says it's made of some kind of metal called brass. It sure shines pretty. Maybe you can get one for me someday as a present. That'd be nice of you, you being kin and all."

Fargo decided to veto his stomach and go.

Just then Beaumont glanced down the valley. "Say, what's goin' on?"

The thunder of hooves broke the morning stillness. Riders were coming, a lot of them, at a gallop.

"That can't be good," Beaumont said.

"No," Fargo agreed. It couldn't.

# 20

The timber was so heavy that Fargo didn't get a good look at the riders until they swept out of the woods into the clearing.

Lester had brought his rifle out and was ready to shoot but held his fire. "Why, it's my brothers and my cousins. What in tarnation brings them here so early in the day and in such a hurry?"

They had all come: Granville, Rufus, Vernon, and Solomon. Along with some of their oldest sons.

Granville was out of the saddle before his horse stopped moving. Running up to Lester, he said, "Have you seen them? Tell me you've seen some sign of them."

"Of who?" Lester asked in confusion.

Granville turned to Fargo. "They took her. Last night, it must have been, but we didn't notice until this mornin'. She likes to go out and admire the stars, and that must be when they grabbed her."

"Grabbed who, consarn it?" Lester demanded.

"Darlene."

"What? Who was it took her?"

"Who else, damn it?" Granville said. "The outlaws."

"But that can't be," Lester said. "They attacked my place last night. Fargo here took on the whole pack and drove 'em off."

"It wasn't the whole pack," Fargo said. "Two were missing."

Granville was a study in misery. "Then those are the two who must have done it. You were right. It's not just money or horses they're after."

"The mangy bastards," Lester said.

The others had stayed on their horses. Rufus leaned on his saddle horn and said, "We're wastin' daylight. Are you goin' to ask him or not?"

Granville turned to Fargo. "We tried to track them but lost the sign. You might be better at it, you bein' a scout and all. I'm beggin' you. Will you come have a look?"

Fargo was more than happy to get away from Periwinkle and her matrimonial shenanigans. "I'll fetch my horse." He hurried to the corral, undid the Ovaro's reins, and was about to fork leather when Periwinkle came up.

"You weren't fixin' to ride off without sayin' good-bye, were you?"

"Your cousin's life is in danger."

"I know that. But I wouldn't mind a hug to tide me over until I see you again."

"Are you and your cousin close?"

"Darlene? Why, sure. We're like two peas in a pod. Why?"

"Nothing." Fargo gave her a quick squeeze, stepped into the stirrups, and reined the stallion around.

"Be careful, you hear?" Periwinkle said. "Anything happens to you, I'll be crushed the rest of my born days."

Fargo's stomach rumbled again and he mentally told it to go to hell. Gigging the Ovaro, he rode to the front of the cabin.

Granville was in the saddle and anxious to depart.

"I wish I could come with you," Lester said. "But with my leg like it is, I can't hardly ride."

"You stay and watch over your family," Granville said. "I'll leave my oldest boy with you to help. He offered to on his own accord and it's a good idea."

The oldest son, Fargo noticed, gave Periwinkle a longing look as she came back around. *Good,* he thought. Maybe the boy could get her to fall for him instead.

A few more words and the Tennesseans were off, thundering down the valley as they'd come up it.

The cool of the morning wouldn't give way to the heat of the summer's day for an hour or so. They passed clearing after clearing, cabin after cabin. Women and children waved and once a dog chased them partway and turned back.

Granville's wife, Charlotte, was outside waiting with her brood. Her eyes were moist and she was wringing her hands. As her husband alighted and led Fargo to the side of the cabin, she remarked, "There's been no sign of anyone."

"This is where my girl usually comes," Granville said, leading Fargo to a spot between the cabin and the trees.

Fargo didn't see what made it so special. He surveyed the sky, aware that more dark clouds had gathered to the northwest and seemed to be hovering there, like troops waiting for reinforcements. He turned in a circle and realized much of the western and southern sky with all their stars would be open to Darlene's gaze at night.

Turning his attention to the ground, Fargo crouched. The grass was crumpled flat. A trail of bent blades led to the trees. Moving slowly, the Ovaro's reins in his hands, he told them, "She had her back to the woods. Two men snuck up on her."

"How can you tell?" Rufus asked. "I don't see a damn thing."

"See here?" Fargo pointed at some marks. "Their weight was on the balls of their feet and they were taking short steps. They must have gotten a hand over her mouth and carried her off."

"Carried her?" Granville said.

Fargo nodded. "See where this heel digs in?" He reached the forest and discovered even more sign. It brought him to where the pair had tied their horses. "There's sign of a struggle," he informed them. "They must have gagged and tied her and she fought back."

"Good for her," Vernon said. "That gal of yours is a scrapper, Granville."

Granville didn't reply.

"They threw her over one of the horses," Fargo continued, "then walked their animals away." He continued for another forty yards. "Here's where they climbed on. They must have figured no one would hear them gallop off." He pointed. "They headed east."

"Toward the lake," Granville said.

Fargo considered it unlikely the outlaws would go there with the cavalry patrol camped along the shore.

"If they've harmed her . . . ," Granville said, and didn't finish.

As Fargo once again swung onto the stallion, he had a thought that gave him pause.

"What are you waitin' for?" Granville asked impatiently. "Lead the way and we'll be right behind."

"You might not want to take so many," Fargo said.

It was Rufus who answered him. "Why in hell not? There are seven of those no-accounts."

"It might not just be Darlene they're after."

"What are you sayin'?" Vernon said.

"All of you have daughters, some about the same age as Darlene." Fargo glanced at Charlotte, who had followed them, along with several of the children. "All of you have wives."

Granville blanched. "God Almighty. I'm so worried about Darlene I wasn't thinkin'. He's right. We need to have a man or one of the grown boys at each cabin. Solomon, you'll stay and see to that. Vern and Rufus and me will go."

"What if there's gunplay?" Solomon objected. "That's not enough of you."

"It will have to be," Granville said. He looked at Fargo. "What do you say? Will the three of us do or should I bring more?"

Fargo grinned and said, "Let's go kill us some sons of bitches."

# 21

The trail was plain enough. Too plain. Darlene's abductors had made no attempt to hide their tracks.

"That don't sound right," Rufus commented when Fargo brought it up. "What do you reckon they're up to?"

"Could be they're hopin' we'll ride into an ambush," Vernon said.

Fargo was thinking the same thing. The little he'd seen of the man called Latham had shown that he was as crafty as they came. "Keep your eyes peeled," he advised. "Anything out of the ordinary, tell me right away."

"These damn sidewinders," Rufus spat. "Why can't they just let folks like us be?"

"You know the answer to that," Granville said. "It's because they *are* sidewinders. Rattlers can't help biting. It's what they do."

"Maybe so," Rufus said. "But rattlers don't go lookin' for folks to bite. They lie around mindin' their own business until you step on them. Human sidewinders ain't the same."

The tracks led along the east side of the valley, hugging the curves of the mountains.

"They're fightin' shy of the cabins," Vernon observed.

"In case your gal lets out a holler, I bet," Rufus said.

As Fargo expected would be the case, the tracks led them to where the two who took Darlene had joined up with the five who attacked Lester's place. They'd sat their horses awhile, apparently talking, then ridden up the mountain behind them.

"These bad men are lunkheads," Rufus said. "Climbin' will slow their horses. We maybe can catch up before the sun goes down."

"Let's hope," Granville said.

At the first ridge, the outlaws had reined to the south.

"Why, look at this," Rufus said. "They're headin' back the way they came. What kind of sense is that?"

"They must figure they'd be less likely to be spotted up here," Granville speculated.

"Seems stupid to me," Rufus said.

Preoccupied with the tracks, Fargo looked up when a shadow fell across him.

A mass of gray and black clouds were scuttling across the sky like so many aerial crabs. At the same moment a cool breeze buffeted him.

"Looks as if it's fixin' to rain," Vernon remarked.

Fargo wasn't so sure. The clouds didn't appear all that moisture-laden. There might be a cloudburst or two, but that would be it. Which worked in their favor. A heavy rain would erase the tracks.

Granville became more agitated the farther they went. He couldn't sit still. He fidgeted. He rose in the stirrups. He tapped his fingers on his saddle horn.

"If you're not careful, brother," Vernon said, partly in jest, "you're liable to have a conniption."

"If she was your girl you'd be the same," Granville growled. "If they've harmed a hair on her head or had their way with her, I swear—"

"Talk like that won't help much," Vernon said.

"If it was me," Rufus said, "I'd be thinkin' on how I'm goin' to splatter their brains. My girls are the sweetest this side of anywhere, and if anything were to happen to them, I'd go plumb berserk."

Fargo shut out their jabber. The outlaws had taken to a game trail and wound single file up a steep slope. On either side towered tall firs. They were so high they blotted out much of the light that the clouds didn't. A preternatural twilight gloom fell, even though it was the middle of the day.

It was ideal for an ambush.

Fargo rode with his hand on his Colt, but they made it out the other side without incident.

By now they were half a mile or more above the valley floor. From their vantage many of the clearings and cabins were visible.

"Why, my family looks like ants down there," Rufus remarked.

The trail climbed higher.

To Fargo it made no sense. There was nothing up there but more timber. Unless the outlaws knew of a pass to the other side, the climb was pointless.

Then the forest thinned and a boulder field appeared.

Fargo's suspicions flared. He drew rein under the last of the trees and scanned the jumble of big boulders, small boulders, stone slabs, and more that lay as if scattered by the hand of a giant.

"What are we waitin' for?" Granville asked.

"Look before you leap," Fargo said.

"Are we frogs now?" Rufus said, and snickered.

"I don't aim to sit here all day," Granville said. "Either it's safe or it isn't. How about if I go on ahead? If I make it to the top, you can follow."

"I'll go," Fargo volunteered. Clucking to the Ovaro, he looked for where the tracks continued. It was hopeless. Horses were heavy, but even they couldn't leave sign on solid rock. His best bet was to pick up the tracks again on the other side.

He took his time. The climb was treacherous. One slip and the Ovaro might break a leg.

About midway, Fargo spied a single track. He skirted a slab that must be fifteen feet high, and down below the Tennesseans commenced to shout and bellow like madmen. All three were pointing above him.

Fargo looked up.

Latham and another man had come out of hiding and wedged long poles under a boulder.

The reason was obvious.

They were about to cause a rock slide.

# 22

A spike of dread shot through Fargo. He wouldn't have time to rein around and reach the bottom before the boulders caught him and the Ovaro. All it would take was one lucky hit and the stallion would suffer a broken leg, or worse.

Twisting in the saddle, Fargo yanked the Henry from the scabbard. He levered a cartridge into the chamber, pressed the stock to his shoulder, and took aim. Latham was partially hidden by the boulder the pair were trying to dislodge, but the other man wasn't.

Fargo sent a slug through his chest. The outlaw dropped his tree limb, clutched himself, and staggered. Fargo fired again and the man dropped.

Latham was furiously striving to get the boulder rolling. His shoulder was pressed to the limb, his body a taut bow.

Fargo worked the Henry's lever, fixed a quick bead, and stroked the trigger. He saw the spark of the slug ricocheting off the boulder. Latham ducked, then thrust his shoulder at the limb again. Fargo fired twice more, each ricochet closer than the last. Suddenly letting go of the limb, Latham sprinted for the woods. Fargo fired yet again. This time the spark was at Latham's boot heels.

Some of the other outlaws came to Latham's aid, opening up with their rifles, and lead whizzed uncomfortably near the Ovaro.

Fargo sprayed shots from the Henry as fast as he could work the lever. Down below, the Tennesseans joined in. Their single-shot rifles had more range than the repeaters the outlaws were using, and they were seasoned backwoodsmen who could shoot the head off a turkey or drop a duck on the wing. Fargo's and their combined fusillade caused the outlaws to melt away.

Latham was the last to disappear. He stopped and defiantly glared at Fargo as if daunting him to try again.

Fargo took quick aim.

Smirking, Latham gestured and was gone.

Fargo fired anyway. It was a waste of lead but he was mad.

The clatter of hooves told him the Tennesseans were coming to join him. He didn't take his eyes off the trees above. At any hint of movement, he'd shoot. But the outlaws didn't reappear and presently his three companions drew rein on either side.

"They almost had you," Granville said.

"We can cover each other better by stickin' together," Vernon said. "So here we are."

"Besides which, we're grown men and do as we darn well please," Rufus threw in.

"Did I see you drop one of the buzzards?" Granville asked.

"You did," Fargo said.

"Reckon he's dead?"

"Let's go see."

The outlaw lay sprawled with his legs bent under him, his chest marked by two large scarlet stains.

"Who was he?" Rufus wondered.

"No idea," Fargo said.

"Good riddance, I say," Vernon declared. "Now there are only six."

"Six is more than four," Rufus said.

"Our four is more than enough," Vernon said, "when three of them are us and we have the scout to track."

"Let's not get cocky," Granville warned. "Not when it's my girl's life that's at stake."

"You reckon I don't know that?" Vernon said.

A gust of wind caused Fargo to glance up. Clouds covered the entire sky, but so far not a single drop of rain had fallen.

As if to prove him wrong, to the northwest thunder rumbled.

"Just what we don't need," Rufus said. "The rain will wash away their tracks."

"Then why are we sittin' here?" Granville demanded.

Fargo pushed on. Once again the outlaws made no attempt to throw them off. The tracks led south for half a mile. From there, the outlaws had headed down the mountain.

"Look at these jokers," Rufus said. "Ridin' all helter-skelter. Do they even know where they're goin'?"

"I don't like that they're headin' back down to our valley," Granville said.

"Hell, we killed one and put the fear of God into them," Rufus declared. "They're runnin' for their lives is what they're doin."

"I wouldn't take these jaspers lightly," Vernon said. "Everythin' they do has a purpose."

Fargo agreed. Latham wasn't the kind to run off with his tail tucked between his legs. Likely as not, Latham had another ambush in mind. When and where were the questions.

Descending a mountain was always easier than climbing one. They rode faster. Judging by the tracks, the outlaws were riding faster, too.

Now and again Fargo heard a distant roll of thunder, but he paid it no mind. Saving Darlene was all that mattered. He regretted not going for Captain Benson and the patrol the day before. If he had, the outlaws might have thought twice about attacking the settlers and Darlene would be safe.

They came to a bench and drew rein to rest their lathered mounts.

"We ain't far behind," Rufus said. "We'll have them before long, or my name ain't Rufus T. Calloway."

"We couldn't have done it without you," Granville said to Fargo. "You're a far better tracker than any of us."

"I've had a lot of experience," Fargo said while studying the forest below.

"You ride mighty well and shoot mighty well, too," Granville said.

Rufus snickered. "Marry him, why don't you?"

Vernon laughed.

"Are all scouts as handy as you are?" Granville asked.

"Some," Fargo said.

"Are you in love?" Rufus teased.

"Cut it out," Granville snapped. "All I'm sayin' is that I used to think these army scouts weren't nothin' but fancy Daniel Boones, what with their buckskins and long hair and all." He nodded at Fargo. "This here gent is the real article. And if the army is smart enough to hire hellions like him, maybe those bluecoats are smarter than we thought they were."

"Speaking of the army," Fargo brought up, "I'm going to have to tell them about you sooner or later."

"Granville told us what you told him about that patrol," Vernon said. "Who do they think they are, comin' all this way to tell us we can't settle where we want?"

"They might let you stay," Fargo said.

"I'm not leavin' for no one," Rufus declared. "Not the army nor God Almighty."

"Don't blaspheme," Granville said.

"You'll jinx us," Vernon said.

"Hell," Rufus said, and raised his reins. "How about we catch up to these varmints and end this?"

"How about we do?" Fargo said.

# 23

They came on a dead horse half an hour later.

It had fallen and crashed to the ground, sliding another twenty feet or more. A front leg was broken. Now it lay in a pool of blood. Instead of shooting it to put it out of its misery, the outlaws had slit its throat.

"Poor critter," Rufus said. "I can't stand to see a horse hurt."

"Me, either," Fargo said. Climbing down, he read the sign. "It tripped in that rut." He pointed at a fold in the ground, covered with pine needles. "When it went down, it spilled two people, not one." He showed them where the grass and brush had been flattened in two places.

"One must have been Darlene," Granville exclaimed in alarm. "She could have broken her neck."

Fargo bent to Darlene's tracks. "She was limping when she got up. See how one foot bears down more than the other and leaves a deeper track?"

"If you say so, mister," Rufus said. "To me, tracks are tracks. I can't read 'em like you."

Fargo studied the boot prints of the outlaw who'd been thrown. "I think Latham was the rider. Here's where he paced back and forth, probably cussing a mean streak."

"I'll show him 'mean' when we catch up," Granville growled.

Again they pushed on. They hadn't descended a quarter of a mile when they came to a grassy shelf and drew sharp rein.

"I'll be!" Rufus exclaimed.

Another body lay in the grass, the man's face contorted in the agony he had felt when he died, a beaver hat lying beside his head.

"Hagler," Fargo said.

But it was the person seated on a log, who looked up and smiled wearily, that astonished them.

"Howdy, Pa. It took you long enough," Darlene said. Her hair was a mess and her nightgown was torn and her face was set in lines of pain.

"Daughter!" Granville cried. Scrambling from his saddle to her side, he hugged her. "Oh, gal, gal," he said huskily, tears filling his eyes. "You had me worried plumb sick. If anything had happened to you, I'd never forgive myself."

"You can't blame yourself for what those outlaws did," Darlene said. "That's just silly."

"It was me who wanted to move out here from Tennessee," Granville said. "It was me talked the rest of you into it."

"We all made up our own minds," Vernon said.

"That's right," Rufus said. "You put it to a vote and we voted. So if anybody is to blame, it's all of us."

"That's silly, too," Darlene said.

Fargo climbed down to examine Hagler. The outlaw hadn't been dead long, but he reeked. Apparently he hadn't believed in baths. A bullet hole in the ribs explained why he was lying there.

"You shot him at Lester's place, or so they told me," Darlene said over her father's shoulder. "He's been in pain the whole time I was with them. Toward the end, he couldn't hardly sit his saddle. When he finally fell off, he lay there beggin' Latham to help him. All Latham did was cuss."

"I'd like to run into that galoot," Rufus said.

"No, Uncle," Darlene said. "You wouldn't. He's scary. It's his eyes. Lookin' into them is like lookin' into hellfire."

"I can be scary, too," Rufus said.

Vernon was staring at Hagler. "Now there are only five. We've evened up the odds a mite."

"One of them is hurt," Darlene said. "Kline, his name is. He got hit in the shoulder and can't use a rifle, but he can use his pistol all right." She, too, stared at Hagler. "It's why they left me with the body and skedaddled. I was slowing them down."

"It's a miracle," Granville said.

"No, Pa," Darlene said. "It's that Latham. He said with only four of them able to fight, he wasn't takin' any chances. He figured that if he hurt me, you wouldn't stop huntin' him this side of the grave. So he left me here."

Granville swiped his sleeve at his nose. "Fargo says you were limpin' when that horse fell."

"It happened so suddenlike," Darlene replied. "I tried to jump clear but sprained my leg. It hurts some and slows me when I walk. Latham didn't like that, neither. He said . . ."

"Said what, girl?" Granville prodded when she didn't go on.

"He said that pokin' me wouldn't be as much fun with me hurt. He said that he wasn't hankerin' to do it no more. That I wasn't worth what it had cost him."

"I'll kill him dead someday," Granville vowed.

Darlene focused on Fargo. "It's you he's afeard of. He said you're a hellion. That you shot three of them and killed two. And when it comes to trackin', you're like a bloodhound on a scent. He wanted nothin' more to do with you."

"Don't that beat all?" Rufus grinned at Fargo. "I wish bad men were as afraid of me as they are of you."

Darlene looked exhausted. She had smudges of dirt on her face from her fall, and when she shifted her legs, she winced.

"We should get her home," Fargo suggested.

"Eh?" Granville said, and blinked. "Damn me for a fool. I'm so happy, I'm not thinkin' straight." He held out his hand. "Come on, girl. He's right. We'll get you back to your ma, so she can fuss over you."

Vernon peered down the mountain. "Where did Latham and them others get to?"

"He said they're leavin' this neck of the country," Darlene said. "He said he wants to get miles away from him." She pointed at Fargo.

Rufus laughed and happily smacked his leg. "I'll be switched. All's well that ends well. Isn't that what folks say?"

To the northwest, more thunder rumbled.

# 24

As Rufus described it, their celebration was to the "humdinginest joviality since who flung the chunk."

Word was spread, and everyone was to gather at Granville's cabin. Each family was to bring food and drink—"especially drink," Rufus said—and they would eat and drink and make merry over the deliverance of Granville's daughter and the defeat of the outlaws.

Fargo was invited. He'd debated for all of two minutes over whether he would stay for the festivities or ride to Flathead Lake and inform Captain Benson that he'd found the settlers. Another night wouldn't make any difference. He decided to stay.

The Tennesseans were in grand spirits. Once Darlene had been tended to, the family prepared for the frolic. They carried their table outside and set the chairs out. Charlotte and the girls busied themselves cooking and baking while the boys scurried about under Granville's watchful eye.

Fargo was left on his own. He offered to help, but his host wouldn't hear of it.

"You've done saved my girl, and that's no lie," Granville declared. "You just take it easy and let us do the work."

To Fargo's delight, Granville went down in their root cellar and came back out with a bottle of whiskey.

"Made it my own self before we left Tennessee," Granville informed him. "Since you're a drinkin' man, I figured you could get an early start while we're busy gettin' ready."

"You're a gentleman and a scholar, as they say," Fargo said, accepting it.

"A what, now?"

"He means he's grateful, Pa," Darlene said, coming up. She used her sprained foot lightly, and was limping. Washed and scrubbed, she now wore a homespun dress and had tied a red ribbon in her hair.

"You two jaw some while I get to work," Granville said, and left them.

"Your pa is a good man," Fargo remarked.

"One of the best," Darlene said with a fond smile. She pulled out a chair, eased down, and indicated one for him.

"Don't mind if I do." Opening the bottle, Fargo sat and tipped it to his mouth. He chugged lustily, several swallows of some of the smoothest moonshine this side of anywhere. "Nice," he said when he lowered the bottle.

"Goodness gracious," Darlene said. "My uncles can't hardly take a sip without coughin'. You must be awful used to liquor."

"Had my share," Fargo said.

"So that's two things I know you're fond of."

Fargo glanced over, thinking that she was poking fun at him. But her expression was serious, and there was a hint of something else in her gorgeous eyes. "You shouldn't bring that up."

"Why not?" Darlene replied, and laughed. "Are you shy about it?"

"What do you think?"

"I think you're not shy about anything. I think when you see somethin' or someone you hanker after, you go after it or her and don't let anyone stand in your way."

Taking another swig, Fargo smacked his lips.

"Am I right?" Darlene asked.

Fargo shrugged. "Doesn't much matter, does it? You're hardly in any condition after what you've been through."

"What do you know of my condition? I have a sprained leg, is all. Or were you plannin' to make love to it and not the rest of me?"

Fargo laughed so loud that some of the kids, and Granville, stopped what they were doing to glance over.

"Careful," Darlene teased. "Your lust is showin'."

"You're saying you're still interested?"

"I never wasn't. You're about the most handsome figure of a man I've ever set eyes on."

Fargo thought of Periwinkle. "Hold on. Just so we're clear. You're not looking for a husband, are you?"

"I'm single," Darlene said. "Single gals are always lookin' to be hitched. But don't you worry. I wouldn't ever say 'I do' to you."

Fargo didn't know whether to be relieved or offended. "Is there something wrong with me?"

"My ma taught me to see people as they are and not as I think they are. Some gals might look at you, at how handsome you are, and that's all they'd see. They'd want you for your good looks and nothin' else." Darlene paused. "Me, I have higher standards. When I finally take a man into my bed, permanent, I want him to be devoted to me and nothin' else. I don't want a drinker. I don't want a cardplayer. And I don't want someone so handsome he'll have to beat other females off with a club."

"Well, hell," Fargo said.

"Nothin' personal," Darlene said. "Truth is, I like you as you are. You'll do for an hour under the stars, but no more."

Placing a hand on his chest, Fargo said, "You'd make love to me and throw me aside?"

Darlene laughed. "Men do that all the time. Now the shoe is on the other foot. So I should ask. Are *you* still interested?"

"Is the sun up in the sky?" Fargo joked.

"No," Darlene said.

Fargo had forgotten about the clouds. They stretched from horizon to horizon. Every so often thunder pealed, but he never saw lightning. And the air didn't feel right for rain. "I'm interested, sun or no sun."

"Tonight you might have your chance," Darlene said quietly. "Just don't let my folks catch on. They'd be powerful disappointed in me. Ma in particular. She's always goin' on about how a woman should save herself."

"I'll leave it up to you," Fargo said. "When the time is right, you let me know."

"What a gallant gent you are."

"No," Fargo said. "I'm randy."

Darlene burst out cackling but put a hand over her mouth. "You're not supposed to come right out with it."

"It's not as if you don't know I want to peel off that dress and run my hands all over you."

A flush spread from Darlene's neck to her forehead. "Careful," she said. "We'll give it away."

"You're the one blushing."

"I can't help it. I've only ever done *that* a few times. The last was with a fella back to Tennessee who was always goin' on about how he wanted us to be man and wife. He courted me for pretty near a year. But when he found out Pa wanted to head out west and I asked him to come along, do you know what he said?"

"I wasn't there."

"He said 'No, thanks.' That he wasn't about to be turned into a pincushion with arrows on my account."

"True love," Fargo said.

"Someday, maybe," Darlene said wistfully. "For now I keep my eyes skinned for the right fella, and now and then when a good-lookin' rascal like you comes along, I let him remind me why I'm lookin' for that right fella in the first place."

"Lucky me," Fargo said.

# 25

One by one the families arrived until the corral was filled with horses to overflowing. The extras were tied to the outside of the corral rails.

There was enough food to gag all the horses. When the Tennesseans celebrated, they went at it with a zest Fargo admired.

Since their vegetable gardens hadn't produced much yet, a lot of the fare was meat. Hunters all, they'd stocked their larders full with deer and elk and rabbit and more.

The wives had no objection to their menfolk drinking on an occasion like this, and the men made the most of it. From their secret stocks they brought whiskey distilled in the hills of Tennessee.

Fargo gorged on more home cooking. He started with a slab of elk meat, dripping with juice, and potatoes and carrots. When cooked right, and this was, elk meat didn't have the gamy taste that deer meat did. He smeared butter on the potatoes and carrots and sprinkled both with salt. His first bite made his mouth water.

Normally at table the Tennesseans were quiet, but not now. The children, in particular, made the most of the occasion by keeping up a constant whirl of chatter and giggles and laughs.

Several times Fargo caught Darlene giving him pointed looks. They boded well for later.

Unfortunately Periwinkle was giving him pointed looks, too. She had walked over to him when the family arrived and looked up as if expecting a hug and a kiss. All he said was "Howdy." When she asked if something was the matter, he told her they needed to talk after the meal.

For dessert he had his choice from four pies and a cake. He couldn't decide between a slice of apple and a slice of cherry, so he had a slice of both.

Usually he would wash it all down with coffee, but today he washed it down with whiskey.

It was about the most perfect meal he'd ever eaten.

When the sun set, they didn't see it. Clouds still covered the entire sky. Thunder occasionally rumbled, but Fargo never saw lightning.

As the women were clearing the dishes and the men were breaking out pipes and cigars, Fargo rose to stretch his legs. He took his glass with him and strolled to where he had an unobstructed view of the sky. Miles off, there was a flash of light, high up in the clouds. Heat lightning, folks called it.

"I hope it doesn't rain and spoil things," Periwinkle said behind him.

Fargo hadn't heard her come up.

Periwinkle had on her best dress and a bonnet. She was wringing her hands and had a worried look in her eyes. "Somethin' is wrong. I can tell. Don't keep me in suspense. I can't stand it."

"I like you," Fargo began. "You're a fine woman, Periwinkle Calloway."

"There's a 'but' comin'," she said. "I just know it."

Fargo had already worked out what he was going to say to lessen the sting. "I had a lot of time to think with all that riding today. And I figure I should be honest with you."

"Oh God," Periwinkle said.

"I'm not ready to take a wife. If I gave you that idea, I didn't mean to. I should have made it plainer. I'm sorry, but we won't ever be man and wife."

Periwinkle wasn't devastated at all. Instead she nodded and said, "I've had time to think, too. I realized I was being forward. I saw that what you were really interested in was my body."

Fargo braced himself for a slap to the face.

"And I decided that's all right."

"What?"

"I talked it out with myself and I would like it very much if you would take me and have your way with me."

"What the hell?"

"Why do you sound upset? That's what you've wanted all along, isn't it?" Periwinkle paused. "A girl always has her first time. I figure I could do a lot worse than have my first time be you."

"But—"

Periwinkle put a finger to his lips. "That's all right. It surprised me, too, my feelin's for you. I'm just lettin' you know that if you want me, I won't say no." She removed her finger.

"Listen, girl," Fargo said, "maybe you should think this out more and—"

"No," Periwinkle cut him off. "I've thought about it until my head hurts. It's what I want. I honestly and truly do. Look me up later and you can ravish me to your heart's content."

"Have you been drinking?"

"No. Why would you even ask that?" Periwinkle smiled serenely and put her palm to his cheek. "Be gentle with me. You'll be my first and I want it to be somethin' I'll remember forever. Can you do that?"

"Periwinkle, listen—"

She stepped back. "That's all right. It must shock you, me throwin' myself at you this way. The truth is, I've shocked myself. I've never had the kinds of thoughts about a man that I've been havin' about you. I get hot all over, and sweaty, and I hardly ever sweat. And I get prickly where I've never felt prickly before."

"Prickly?"

"So don't keep me waitin' too long, you hear? After the music commences and everyone is dancin' and whoopin' is when you should come find me. They'll never notice when we slip off." Periwinkle leaned toward him to whisper, "And, Skye?"

Fargo was half-afraid to ask. "What?"

"I'm not wearin' a stitch under this dress."

"Oh hell."

Periwinkle smiled and walked away, swaying her hips as she had never swayed them before.

Fargo drained his glass in two gulps, and coughed. He glanced at the sky and saw another crackle of heat lightning. In need of a refill, he went to the table and was about to pour when Darlene walked past and gave him another of her "I want you" looks.

"Later, handsome."

Fargo watched her sashay off. "How do I get myself into these things?"

# 26

Night fell, and while heat lightning stroked the clouds above, the Tennesseans danced their hearts out, wheeling and spinning, sometimes arm in arm and at other times between two lines of dancers who took turns cavorting down the center.

Lester was a fine fiddle player. Vernon played a washboard, using a tin cup. Rufus drummed on an overturned tub.

It was their first big to-do since leaving Tennessee, and they were so caught up in the fun and drink that no one noticed when Darlene approached Fargo and put her mouth close to his ear.

"Meet me out back of the corral in about five minutes."

Fargo was clapping to the beat of the music, and nodded. He felt her finger run across the back of his neck. When, not a minute later, he felt the finger again, he said, "You're still here?" He looked over his shoulder.

It was Periwinkle. "I'm what?"

"Oh," Fargo said.

Periwinkle rose onto her toes so her lips brushed his ear. "Slip around to the side of the cabin in ten minutes or so. I'll be waitin'."

Fargo opened his mouth to say, "Hold on," but she had already turned and was walking off. To make himself heard over the music he'd have to shout, and that would draw attention.

Periwinkle glanced back and gave a little wave.

"What to do?" Fargo said. He could have Darlene or he could have Periwinkle. Choosing one was bound to make the other mad if she found out about it. He could be smart and not have anything to do with either. But women were like whiskey. He never said no to a bottle and he never said no to a willing filly.

"What to do?" Fargo asked himself again.

"About what?"

Fargo nearly jumped.

Charlotte Calloway had come over and was reaching now for his arm. "How about a dance?"

"Your husband won't mind?"

"It was Granville's idea," Charlotte replied. "He saw you standin' over here by your lonesome and said it's a shame you're not havin' fun like the rest of us." She gazed about them. "I'd have you dance with Darlene, but I don't see her anywhere. Or Lester's girl, Periwinkle. She likes to dance, too. But she's not around, neither. So I guess you'll have to settle for me." She took his hand and pulled him out to the space cleared for dancing.

Some of her kin whooped and Rufus hollered, "Stomp your boots off, Fargo!"

Fargo raised her arm and launched into a barn dance he was familiar with. He didn't dance all that often. Most of his courting, if you could call it that, was done in saloons and houses of ill repute where the ladies didn't need to be dined and danced with before they'd let a man kiss them.

Charlotte cheerfully and gracefully went through the moves, matching him nicely, and they weren't halfway through when everyone was clapping and stamping their feet in time to the music.

Fargo was mildly surprised that he was enjoying himself so much. When the dance ended and Charlotte asked him to do another, he agreed without thinking.

This one was slower, more English-style, and involved a lot of turning back and forth and both of them holding their arms aloft at certain points, and Charlotte doing a lot of curtseying.

About halfway through, he happened to catch sight of Periwinkle by the table, watching. He'd taken so long, she'd come back to see why. And damned if she didn't look jealous.

The dance came to an end and Rufus called out the next one. In the swirl of the dancers taking position and changing partners, Fargo thanked Charlotte and slipped away on the opposite side from Periwinkle. She was pouring herself some tea and didn't spot him.

Once he reached the corral and no one could see him, Fargo ducked and ran. He thought that maybe Darlene had given up on him, but there she was, bathed in starlight, beauty in a dress.

"Took you long enough."

"Your mother asked me to dance."

Darlene grinned. "That would be my ma. She loves to dance more than anything. Back to Tennessee, Pa had to drag her home whenever they went to a social, she loves it so much."

"She said it was his idea," Fargo mentioned, glancing back.

For all he knew, Periwinkle might have spotted him and followed. He saw no sign of her.

"Most of his ideas are really hers," Darlene said. "Moving out here was one of them. She never could cotton to a lot of people livin' close to her 'less'n they were kinfolk. She's devoted to our family, but everyone else is an outsider."

Fargo thought of the Apaches, who put their band and their people before all else, and to whom everyone else was an enemy. "Why are we standing here talking about her when there's strolling to do?"

Darlene snickered. "Is that what you want to do? Stroll?"

For an answer, Fargo pulled her close, molding her bosom to his chest and her thighs to his. "What do you think?"

Laughing, Darlene pushed him back. "I think you'd better hold your horses until we're not out in the open. My pa or my ma spot us, they won't take it kindly—you seducin' their sweet, innocent daughter."

Fargo snickered and clasped her hand. "Follow me."

"No, you follow me," Darlene said. "I know these woods better than you, and I have the perfect spot."

Fargo was vaguely aware of more heat lightning. As they were about to enter the benighted forest, far to the northwest an actual bolt of lightning cleaved the heavens, so vivid and bright he had the illusion he could reach out and touch it.

"Did you see that?" Darlene said in awe. "Looks like we might get some rain, after all."

"Maybe," Fargo said as the thunder drummed. He could barely hear it for the din of the music.

"I've always loved to watch a storm," Darlene said. "Back to home, I'd sit at my bedroom window and watch it rain for hours. The lightnin' and the thunder never scared me any like it does some. I'd love to see more."

"I'd love to see you naked."

Darlene laughed. "About that. We have to be careful, in case someone comes lookin' for me."

Another bolt seared the night, so far off that Fargo counted to ten in his head before he heard the thunder.

"Wasn't that pretty?" Darlene said.

"Not as pretty as you."

"Listen to you," Darlene said, but she was pleased. "But back to our clothes. How do you feel about doin' it with them on? I know naked is better, but it's also takin' a big chance."

"So long as we do it, I don't care if we both wear fur coats."

"In the summer?" Darlene chortled. "I can take a hint. You have one thing and one thing only on your mind. Reckon we should get to it."

"About time," Fargo said.

# 27

Darlene's secret spot was a depression about as long and wide as a horse stall. Matted with pine needles and leaves, it was as soft as a bed. She sat and patted the ground. "What are you waitin' for? An engraved invite?"

"Do I need one?" Fargo asked as he eased down.

They were well hidden. No one could see them unless the person was right on top of them.

"You surely do not," Darlene said, becoming serious. "As handsome as you are, I could eat you alive."

"Start nibbling," Fargo said.

"I'll do more than nibble," Darlene promised, and hungrily locked her mouth to his.

Fargo was treated to a kiss he'd remember. She had a way of moving her lips and using her tongue, as if she really were eating him. She sucked on his and he sucked on hers, and when he leaned back, she was panting.

"That was awful nice," she said.

"You're not going to talk me to death, are you?" Fargo asked. It was one of his peeves. Lovemaking was for lovemaking. Not jabbering.

"I might and I might not. Depends on my mood. Are you fussy about it?" she teased.

"Fussy as hell."

"Now, now. Don't spoil things. Sometimes a little talk helps a gal along. Know what I mean?"

"If you say so," Fargo said. To hush her up, he kissed her again.

This time, his hands explored while their tongues entwined. He roved his fingers from her silken hair to the soft swell of her breasts and down over the flat of her belly. She grew warmer and cooed deep in her throat.

"Yes, sir," Darlene said when they broke for air. "You've done this before."

"There you go again."

"And there you go again," Darlene countered. "There's a time for bein' grumpy, and this ain't it. If I talk a little, forgive me and keep at it." She kissed his cheek. "I wouldn't have taken you for a complainer. Some people, that's all they do. My cousin Periwinkle, for instance."

Fargo scowled. Being compared to Periwinkle was like a sock to the gut. He decided then and there he wasn't mentioning it again.

"Cat got your tongue now?" Darlene taunted playfully.

"No, you do," Fargo said, and stuck it in her mouth. Cupping both breasts, he squeezed, and she melted into him.

The sounds of the music and the thunder faded and her hot moans and groans were all he heard. Hiking up her dress, he discovered she had a chemise on underneath. Hiking that, he ran a hand over a smooth inner thigh and around her leg to cup her rounded bottom. Her gasps became furnaces of unleashed desire as she ground her nether mound into his hardening manhood.

"Yes," she breathed in his ear. "Oh yes."

Kneading her yielding flesh as if it were carnal clay, Fargo incited her more. Her hands were everywhere, exploring every muscle and limb as if she couldn't get enough of him. He nearly gasped himself when her questing fingers found his now-iron pole. She cupped him, low down, and it took every ounce of self-control he possessed not to explode.

Sliding his hand around, he returned the favor by placing his hand between her satiny thighs. His middle finger instantly became wet from the moistness of her nether lips. Inserting it caused her to arch her back and suck in air as if she were about to breathe her last. Instead her voluptuous body erupted in a release of passion as violent as the bucking of a ship on a storm-tossed sea.

Fargo wanted to be in her so much he could taste it. But he held off, using his fingers for a while, stoking her inner fires so when he was ready, she'd be lost in abandon.

Suddenly Darlene smothered an outcry and thrust against his hand as if trying to break it. He felt her spurt, felt her entire body shudder in the ecstasy of release. After a while she sagged against him, her forehead to his chest, catching her breath.

"What you do to me," Darlene said.

"I'm not half-done."

Shifting, Fargo eased on top of her. He slid the folds of her dress and chemise above her hourglass hips, spread her long legs, and reached down to position himself.

At the contact of his tip to her slit, she dug her fingernails into his shoulders and shivered in anticipation.

"Do me," she pleaded. "Oh, do me."

Looking into her lovely eyes, hooded as they were with lust, Fargo smiled and rammed up into her so hard he lifted her bottom off the ground. She instantly wrapped those wonderful legs of hers around his hard body, her heels locked at the small of his back.

Fargo commenced to ride her—in and out, in and out—each measured stroke lofting his own pleasure higher, ever higher, until he was at the pinnacle and had nowhere to go but over the brink.

As if she sensed he was on the cusp, Darlene placed her hot lips to his neck and then his ear and whispered, "Now."

The forest and the night seemed to fade away. His body pumped, and hers was his shadow. Cresting, they eventually slowed to a state of satiated exhaustion. He lay on top of her until she squirmed as if his weight was uncomfortable, and slid onto his side.

"Oh my," Darlene breathed, "that was real nice."

His eyes closed, savoring the feeling of release as he'd savor the finest whiskey, Fargo said, "You can talk now."

Darlene laughed. "I'm almost too tired to."

"Give me ten minutes, and you can have a second helping."

"That soon?" she marveled, and nipped his chin. "I'd like nothin' more, but I can't be gone too long, or my folks might become suspicious, and we wouldn't want that. If my pa found out what we did, as much as he likes you, he'd probably shoot you. We wouldn't want that, either."

"No," Fargo agreed, "we wouldn't."

In the distance thunder boomed.

# 28

Darlene insisted that they stray back separately. Fargo let her go first. He stood at the tree line until she had gone around the corral, and then he ambled toward the near side of the cabin. It didn't occur to him that that was where Periwinkle had told him to meet her, but he remembered right quick when she stepped from the shadows, wringing her hands.

"Well," she said.

Fargo stopped in midstride. With nothing else to say, he responded with "Well, yourself."

"I know what you just did," Periwinkle said accusingly. "I saw my cousin and you go into the woods a while ago."

For some strange reason, the first thing that popped into Fargo's head was "We were picking mushrooms."

"Oh, please. Do you take me for a simpleton? There aren't any mushrooms hereabouts, and you certainly couldn't find any at night without a lantern even if there were."

Fargo didn't know what else to say, so he said nothing. In a way, he was glad she'd seen them. Now she would leave him alone. He just hoped she didn't make trouble for Darlene.

"My cousin always did have a knack for interestin' a fella," Periwinkle said. "Much more so than me."

"Don't hold it against her," Fargo said.

"Oh, I don't. Fact is, I admire her for it. I wish men found me as attractive as they find her."

"You're as pretty as she is," Fargo said. Which wasn't exactly true, but she was close.

"I know what's the matter with me," Periwinkle said. "I've been givin' it a lot of thought for months now, and dang me if I didn't do it again with you."

"Do what?" Fargo asked in mild confusion.

"As soon as you showed an interest, what's the first thing I did?" Periwinkle didn't wait for him to answer. "I started to talk marriage, like I always do when a fella seems to like me. No wonder I scare men off. That's sort of silly, ain't it?"

"Well," Fargo said.

"But thanks to you, I've learned my lesson."

"Me?"

Periwinkle nodded and stepped closer. "Here I was, gettin' all dreamy-headed about marryin' you, and you went off with my cousin. I've got to be practical, like she is, and not be wantin' to marry every handsome fella I see."

"That makes sense," Fargo said.

"Good." Periwinkle beamed. "So, when do you want to?"

"Want to what?"

"Do me like you just did her."

Fargo was dumbfounded.

"Don't look so shocked. I've made it plain I like you. And since I can't have you as my husband, I'd like to have you as the next best thing. You can be my lover."

"Periwinkle, listen," Fargo began. The girl was going from one extreme to the other.

"I'm through listenin' to what others say. I want to do what I want to do, and what I want to do is what Darlene's just done." Periwinkle smiled and put her hand on his. "I'm yours. Do with me as you will."

"You're not thinking straight," Fargo tried.

"For the first time in a long while, I am," Periwinkle insisted sweetly. "Here, I'll prove it."

To Fargo's amazement, she raised his hand and pressed it to her breast.

"How does that feel? I bet it feels as good as hers. I overheard my uncle Rufus say once that menfolk are powerful fond of tits."

Fargo was about to tell her that she needed to get a hold of herself when he felt a familiar hardening below his belt.

"You like it, don't you?" Periwinkle said, and used her fingers to make his fingers squeeze her. "Oh!" she said. "That is nice, ain't it?"

"Girl, you are plumb loco."

"I ain't no girl. I'm a full-growed woman. Do you want to or not? I know you just did it with Darlene, but I overheard my aunt Charlotte say once that men can get randy if all a woman does is wink at him, and you squeezin' me is more than winkin'."

"You overhear too damn much," Fargo said. But she was

right. The feel of her nipple against his palm was causing his pants to bulge.

Periwinkle glanced over her shoulder, then pressed against him. Her face was so close her breath fanned his mouth. "Take me into the woods and ravish me—quick, before somebody comes. What are you waitin' for?"

"My brain to work," Fargo said.

"I don't want your brain. I want this." Periwinkle gripped his pole, making it throb even more, and smiled the knowing smile of a woman who had a man exactly where she wanted him. "I knew it. You want to. If you got any bigger, you'd bust your britches open."

"It would have to be quick," Fargo heard himself say.

"That's all right," Periwinkle said. "Do it however you think best. All I ask is that you transport me to heaven."

That gave Fargo pause. "Do what, now?"

"I heard that somewhere. Heard how doin' it is bliss if it's done right. So do what you have to so I feel as much bliss as I can."

Fargo was beginning to wish they had all night. "Are you sure about this?"

"How many times must I say it? I want to. I want to more than anything. It will be a dream come true."

"It might not be all you expect."

"Let's find out," Periwinkle said.

# 29

Fargo had long ago stopped trying to figure women out. Especially when it came to making love. As best he could figure, they wanted what they wanted when they wanted it, and that was that. There was no talking them out of it once their minds were made up.

The moment the forest closed about them, Periwinkle was on him like a grizzly on honey. She wrapped her arms tight and thrust her face against his. She didn't just kiss him; she devoured him.

"Damn, girl," he said when she drew back. "Take it easy." His lower lip was sore from where she'd mashed it with her teeth.

"I can't help myself," Periwinkle said huskily. "I'm on fire for you." She threw herself at him again.

Scooping her into his arms while kissing her, Fargo carried her to the same spot where he had done it with Darlene. He hoped Darlene didn't wonder what was keeping him and come back, or the two girls might get into an argument over him and maybe bring their parents on the run to find out what the ruckus was about.

As he eased Periwinkle down, she smothered his face and neck with passionate kisses. She licked his ears and sucked on a lobe.

For Fargo's part, he hiked her dress up above her breasts. She made it easier by rising a little while continuing with her mouth and her hands. For a beginner, she had natural talent.

She also had a nice body. Her breasts were ripe melons, her nipples so sensitive that when he pulled one she moaned and fluttered her eyelids. Her silky thatch was a delight to run his fingers through, her smooth-as-marble thighs a treat for his questing palms.

Now that they were committed, he didn't hold back. He did everything he had done with Darlene, and then some. The quickness of it ignited double the fire of need inside him, so that he wanted it as much as Periwinkle did.

And Lordy, how she wanted it. Her hands explored every part of him she could reach. She was particularly fascinated by his member, and stroked and rubbed and fondled it as if it were her new favorite possession. She had a way of gently squeezing the head that made him shiver.

He figured to go a little slower once he was set to penetrate her, but she had other ideas. No sooner did he lightly touch his tip to her slit than she surprised him by looking him in the eye, smiling a secret smile, and impaling herself as adeptly as one of the most high-priced doves in one of the best houses in Denver might do.

Propped on his hands, Fargo held himself still, relishing it.

Not Periwinkle. A volcano of desire, she boiled over. Her mouth was everywhere, her fingers never still. Her pulsing body was as hot as the hottest campfire ember. She didn't wrap her legs around him, as Darlene had done. She placed her feet flat on either side of him and used them as leverage to pump her hips to match his strokes.

Fargo wouldn't have thought she had it in her. But that was the way with women. The quiet, seemingly shy ones were often bundles of surprises.

Periwinkle certainly was. She did things Darlene hadn't done.

Fargo was boiling all over when she went momentarily rigid. With her eyes wide and her mouth parted in an oval of surprise, she looked at him in wonderment and exploded. It was all he could do to stay inside her. She bucked and heaved and thrashed with elemental abandon. Despite the fact that he was so much bigger and must've outweighed her by a hundred pounds, *she* lifted *him* off the ground. Gripping her hips, he enjoyed the ride.

She had said she wanted it to be quick, but after she crested and slowed, she went at him again. Releasing her long-pent-up passion had shattered an inner dam, and now a flood of craving was sweeping all before it.

Fargo had forgotten about everything else, but he was reminded when he heard someone call her name. She heard it, too, because she abruptly stopped and put a finger to his lips. They both listened, but the call wasn't repeated, and she resumed her frantic lovemaking.

Her second explosion and his were simultaneous.

At the end they both collapsed, Periwinkle in the bliss she had sought, Fargo in exhaustion. She had drained him as dry as an empty water skin on a desert trek. He wouldn't be able to do it again for at least an hour.

She dreamily pecked his cheek. "Thank you. It was everything I wanted it to be, and then some."

"Don't spoil it by talking," Fargo said. He'd like to lie there a bit in peace.

"We have to get back," Periwinkle said, sliding to one side and pulling at her dress. "Both of us."

"You first," Fargo said.

"You'll follow right away?" Periwinkle sat up and did more pulling and smoothing.

"Be right behind you."

She bent and kissed him hard on the mouth. "Whenever you want to do it again, let me know. I could do this all day and all night."

"I believe you," Fargo said. Rolling onto his side, he closed his eyes.

"Remember, follow right away."

Fargo heard her move off, heard yet another rumble of thunder in the distance. He supposed he should get up, but he was just too tired. He was on the verge of dozing off when he heard something else: the stealthy rustle of the underbrush.

Instantly he was alert. Since he hadn't undressed, it only took a few moments to hitch at his pants and adjust his gun belt. Palming his Colt, he rolled onto his belly and crawled to the top of the depression.

Silhouettes moved in the nearby woods. He saw several and sensed more.

They seemed to be searching for something.

"Where the hell did they get to, damn it?" one hissed. "We saw them come in here."

"Hush, damn you," another snarled.

Fargo grimly set himself. That last voice was Latham's.

The outlaws had come back.

# 30

Fargo should never have taken it for granted that they had fled. Latham might be a lot of things, none of them decent, but he wasn't yellow.

Another voice, Kline's, whispered, "We're too damn close to that cabin. They might spot us."

"The next one of you who flaps his gums," Latham snarled, "I will kill you where you stand."

The nearest silhouette turned and cat-crept toward Fargo. The man was looking every which way except down.

Fargo didn't so much as twitch until a boot appeared almost in front of his face. Pointing the Colt, he said quietly, "Boo."

The gunman glanced down. His eyes became saucers and he went to point his six-shooter.

Fargo shot him. The slug ripped into the man's gut and on up through his body to burst out where his neck met his shoulder. The impact staggered him and he triggered a shot into the dirt.

Fargo shot him again.

At the blasts, the others went to ground.

Fargo ducked as pistols opened up. They were shooting low, but they didn't realize he was in a hole and their shots were high. In the lull when they'd emptied their cylinders, he rose and fanned a shot at where he believed another of them to be.

The music out by the cabin had stopped. Shouts broke out. Men were coming on the run.

Latham swore, then hollered for his men to scat. Darkling figures darted away.

Fargo rose. He could hear them but didn't see them. He scrambled out and onto his knees, ready to drop if they opened fire. But their rapid footfalls faded even as other steps, from the other direction, grew louder.

"Fargo? Fargo!" Granville bellowed. "Where are you?"

"Here!" Fargo yelled.

Bristling with rifles and shotguns, the Calloways swarmed in and around him.

The sight of the dead man brought exclamations of surprise.

"Ain't that one of those outlaws?" Rufus said, bending to see better.

"I'd wondered where you got to," Granville said to Fargo while raking the woods for their enemies. "Now I know. You must have spotted them or heard somethin' and came for a look-see. Am I right?"

"I got one of them," Fargo said.

"I can see that," Granville replied. "The nerve of those buzzards, comin' back for more."

"We should have known they weren't gone for good," Vernon said.

Solomon nodded. "My gut tells me they'll keep skulkin' around, lookin' to do us harm."

"Let's go after them," Rufus proposed excitedly, "and wipe the bastards out."

"In the dark?" Granville said. "Use your head. We'll hunt for sign in the mornin' and go after them then."

"It will be today all over again," Vernon said. "As much as I want to end this, I've no hankerin' to go ridin' all over creation again."

"What does our scout friend say?" Solomon asked.

Fargo had been pondering. That Latham hadn't lit out when he had the chance was puzzling. Either Latham was out for revenge for the men he'd already lost or something else was at play. "I'll go after them by myself."

"Like blazes you will," Rufus said. "It's our fight, not yours. We're not puttin' it all on you."

"I agree," Granville said.

"What about your families?" Fargo said, and began to reload. "Latham is after something. It can't be your pokes. He has to guess that none of you have a lot of money. And if not that, what?"

"Like you said before," Vernon said grimly, "our womenfolk."

"If he and his men have gone long without, your wives and your daughters would please him more than your pokes."

"They did take Darlene," Lester mentioned, and clutched his crutch. "Why, they might be after my Periwinkle next. And her never havin' been with a man yet. Any of those polecats lays a hand on her, I'll gut him and strangle him with his own innards."

Fargo swore he could feel her burning kisses on his skin as he said, "She's lucky to have a father like you."

Granville nudged the body. "We'll have to bury this gob of spit or it will stink to high heaven before too long."

"Let him stink," Rufus said. "I don't bury those out to do me in."

"So we let him rot this close to my cabin?" Granville said.

"Fine," Rufus spat. "I'll lend a hand so long as we don't bury him deep. An enemy ain't worth that much effort."

Vernon cradled his rifle. "We should call it a night. The festivities are ruined, anyhow. Each of us should head home and snug our families in safe and sound."

"The outlaws could pick some of us off along the way," Lester mentioned.

"Not if we all go together and each of us peels off when we reach our own place," Vernon said.

"That will leave me and mine to cover the last stretch to our cabin by ourselves," Lester said. He turned to Fargo. "Unless you're willin' to ride along. I'm not too proud to ask that you do. You can spend the night like you did before."

Fargo thought of how happy that might make Periwinkle. He

could imagine her sneaking out to be with him and then her father catching them. "I'll do it on one condition."

"Name it," Lester said.

"None of your family is to step foot outside until morning. Your daughter nearly got killed the last time."

"That's easy," Lester said. "I'll bar the door and sleep next to it."

"It's settled, then," Granville said. "Each of you has your family ready to go in fifteen minutes. Let's hope we're wrong and we've seen the last of these owl hoots."

"Wishful thinkin', brother," Rufus said. "Mark my words. The killin' ain't over by a long shot."

"No," Fargo said, "it isn't."

# 31

The wind had picked up as if it were going to storm, but Fargo still didn't smell rain in the air. He hadn't seen any heat lightning in a while, or any of the infrequent bolts.

They came to the second cabin and dropped off Vernon and his brood and moved on toward the third.

Fargo had suggested they ride in single file rather than bunch up, to make it harder for the outlaws to pick them off. The line stretched for a hundred yards or better and he rode up and down it to be sure there weren't any stragglers. As he was returning to the front, Periwinkle motioned.

Bringing the Ovaro up next to her mount, Fargo smiled. Her mother was in front of her and a sister behind and would hear every word. Which was why he said, "What's on your mind, Miss Calloway?"

Periwinkle glanced at her ma. "Not much. I just wanted to talk a little."

"I'm sort of busy."

"Pa told us you'll be spendin' the night again," Periwinkle said, sounding casual about it.

"He's worried about the outlaws." Fargo stated the obvious. "Your family is the farthest in."

"Which puts us in the most danger, I know," Periwinkle said. "You helpin' to protect us means a lot."

"Your family has been kind to me. It's the least I can do."

"Is that the only—" Periwinkle stopped, and pointed. "Say. What's that? Do you see it there, off on the mountain?"

Fargo looked. Miles to the north, well beyond the end of the valley, a thimble-sized orange glow had appeared on a high slope.

"A campfire, you reckon?" Periwinkle speculated, and smacked her leg. "Why, it must be the blamed outlaws."

"They haven't had time to get that far."

"Injuns, then."

"Indians wouldn't give themselves away like that."

"Well, it's sure somebody."

Fargo studied it until a tree blocked his view. Going around, he looked again, but the glow wasn't there.

"I'll be," Periwinkle declared. "Where did it get to?"

Rising in the stirrups, Fargo still didn't see it. That wasn't unusual. At night, at long distances, lights were often will-o'-the-wisps, there one moment and gone the next.

"Keep your eyes peeled and let me know if you see it again," he said.

"I will," she promised.

Fargo kept an eye out, too, but hadn't spotted the light again by the time they reached Lester's cabin. He helped Lester strip the horses of their saddles and saddle blankets while Lester's wife, Priscilla, hustled the children off to bed.

Lester had gone in, and Fargo was about to take a seat with his back to the corral, as he had done the last time, when footsteps pattered and a warm hand slipped into his.

"I'm here," Periwinkle announced.

"No, you're not," Fargo said.

"Yes, I am. You can see me." She rose onto her toes to kiss his chin. "I snuck out so we can do it again."

"No."

"I beg your pardon?"

"Latham is out there somewhere," Fargo reminded her. "Or have you forgotten already?"

"Don't be silly," Periwinkle said peevishly. "How dumb do you think I am?" She grinned and went to press against him, but he was holding the Henry between them and she couldn't. "We can have another quick one."

"And have our throats slit while we're doing it? No, thanks." Truth was, Fargo had often thought that dying while doing it would be a fine way to go.

"How can you let a little thing like that stop you?" Periwinkle asked. "Don't you want me anymore?"

"I'm fond of breathing," Fargo said.

"We can do it and watch for the owl hoots at the same time," Periwinkle said. "It's easy. All we do is keep our eyes open."

How did Fargo argue with logic like that? Fortunately he didn't have to.

Around the cabin limped her father. "Girl? What in blazes are you doin' out there? I told you to get yourself to bed, and I meant it."

Periwinkle jerked her hand from Fargo's as if his were a hot coal. Turning, she smiled sweetly. "I was just checkin' if he needs anything."

"He doesn't," Lester said. "Now get your backside inside. You're too old to paddle but not too old to do extra chores for a month of Sundays if you don't listen and do what you're told."

"Yes, Pa," Periwinkle said contritely. She shot Fargo a look of regret and hurried off.

Lester limped over, grumbling, then said, "Was she tellin' the truth? Did she come out here to see if you needed somethin'?"

Fargo decided he could use the father's help. But he had to be smart about it. "Between you and me, I think she's taken a shine to me."

"The hell you say. What has she done?"

"Nothing yet," Fargo fibbed. "But I can see it in her eyes and how she acts around me. You might want to keep her away from me for her own good. I'd hate to disappoint her."

"I'm obliged for lettin' me know," Lester said. "A lot of men would take advantage of her. That you won't speaks well of your character."

"Don't make more of it than there is."

"You can be humble if you want, but it pleases me I can trust you. There's not a lot of gents I can say that about outside of my kin." Lester smiled and turned to go, and stopped. "What the dickens?"

Fargo looked to the north as Lester was doing. "What did you see?"

"I'm not sure," Lester said. "Some sort of light. It was there and then it wasn't. If I'd blinked, I'd have missed it."

"Periwinkle and I saw one earlier."

"It might have been a campfire, but it looked too big. Lester peered into the night and finally shrugged. "Well, I reckon I should crawl under my own blankets. I'm bushed after the day we had."

"I'll keep watch."

"Don't stay up all night. You have to be as tired as me, what with all the ridin' and whatnot." Lester stretched and yawned and gazed up at the stars. "Lord, I do so love it here."

"I like the wilds, too."

"I mean this valley. It's paradise. Oh, it doesn't rain as much as we'd like, and from what you say, the winters will be like livin' at the North Pole, but it's everything we wanted in our new home, and then some. I can see me spendin' the rest of my days here. My missus feels the same."

Fargo sat and set the Henry across his legs.

"We took a gamble comin' out here and startin' over," Lester said. "Now that we've put down roots again, I'd hate for somethin' to spoil it." He smiled and gave a little wave and limped away.

Fargo settled back. A profound quiet had fallen. Even the horses in the corral were still.

Suddenly a gust of wind buffeted his face. He sniffed but he still didn't smell rain. Instead he caught a whiff of something else.

Smoke.

# 32

The clucking of a raven woke Fargo at the crack of dawn.

He'd stayed awake as long as he could, but there had come a point when his leaden eyelids wouldn't be denied. His chin had drooped to his chest, and he was out like a snuffed candle. He hadn't smelled the smoke again and figured it had been his imagination playing a trick on him.

Now, sitting up, Fargo adjusted his hat. The wind was still strong, and constant. He inhaled and stiffened. This time there was no mistake. His nose tingled with the acrid scent.

Bracing himself against a rail, Fargo stood. The horses still dozed. He gazed to the north but didn't see the light or smoke rising from the forest. But there was no denying the smell.

Overnight, the clouds had dispersed, taking their heat lightning and the occasional bolt with them.

Fargo left the cover of the corral and prowled the perimeter of the clearing.

A squirrel chittered at him. Sparrows frolicked in a thicket. A doe and her fawn eyed him. All signs that no one was skulking about.

He made for the cabin, the Henry's barrel on his shoulder. Lester's wife was usually up early, and she might have coffee on. The smoke he'd smelled could be from the fireplace, although he didn't see any rising from the chimney.

The door opened before he reached it and out slipped Periwinkle. She was looking behind her and didn't see him. Quietly closing the door, she moved toward the side of the cabin.

"Morning," Fargo said.

Periwinkle jumped. Glancing apprehensively at the door, she put a finger to her lips. "Hush, or you'll wake them. No one is up yet. They're sleepin' off last night."

"Too bad," Fargo said. He could really use that coffee.

"No, it's good," Periwinkle said, grabbing his hand, "because now you and me can sneak off and have another of those quick ones."

"Damn, girl."

Periwinkle tugged. "Hurry. We don't have a lot of time. My ma could be up any minute."

Fargo dug in his heels so she couldn't budge him. "I'm not going anywhere and neither are you."

"What's gotten into you?" Periwinkle pulled harder. "I thought you liked makin' love to me. I sure liked makin' love to you. I liked it so much, I want to do it again."

"You say your mother isn't up yet?"

"No, she ain't," Periwinkle said. "So you have nothin' to worry about. Let's go. Please."

"Now's not the time," Fargo said, "and it sure as hell isn't the place."

"The woods are right there," Periwinkle said, pointing.

"And if your mother or father wake up and wonder where we got to and come looking?" Fargo shook his head.

"There won't be a problem if we hurry." Periwinkle pulled harder. "What is the matter with you? Here I am, throwin' myself at you, and you stand there like a bump on a log."

"Wait a minute," Fargo said. "If your mother isn't up yet, where is that smoke coming from?"

"What?" Periwinkle sniffed, and sniffed again. She looked at the chimney and then out over the tiers of timbered slopes. "I smell it, too. Maybe it's blowin' up the valley from one of the other cabins."

"No," Fargo said. "The wind is from the northwest."

"Could it be the outlaws, you reckon?" Periwinkle asked. "From their campfire, maybe?"

"I'll go find out. Let your folks know," Fargo said. If nothing else, it would stop her from pestering him about the other thing. Or so he thought.

"Hold on," she said, catching up. "What's your rush? You can go look for them later. Let's have that quick one."

"Give it a rest."

Periwinkle shook her head in disbelief. "I'm plumb shocked at you turnin' me down."

Fargo was a little shocked himself. He could count the number of times he'd ever said no on one hand and have fingers left over.

"Was it me? Was I no good?"

"You were fine."

"Then why don't you want to? Men are goats. Everybody knows that. My grandma used to say that men can't keep it in their pants if they tried."

"Your grandmother said that?"

"She was a hoot," Periwinkle said fondly. "Married to my grandpa for nigh on fifty years and always teasin' him about that. He'd laugh and say it was a good thing he was so randy because she sure liked it a lot." She stopped. "Wait. Why are we talkin' about them and we should be talkin' about us?" She snatched his hand. "Take me into the trees and ravish me."

"The smoke comes first."

Periwinkle let go. "I'm commencin' to think you don't really like me or that I wasn't as fine as you claim. If you did and I was, you would."

Fargo was tired of her antics. He came to the corral, opened the gate, and entered.

"Don't you beat all?" Periwinkle hung back, her arms folded, angrily tapping her foot. "I have half a mind to tell Pa you had your way with me just so he'll shoot you."

"It was the other way around," Fargo said. "He'd be just as upset at you as he would at me."

"I don't care. I'm so angry I could scream."

Fargo saddled the stallion. He shoved the Henry into the scabbard, led the Ovaro out, and closed the gate. As he went to climb on, Periwinkle clutched at the back of his buckskin shirt.

"Here's an idea. Take me with you a little ways, we'll do it, and then you can go see about the stupid smoke."

"Here's another idea." Fargo smiled. "No way in hell."

Periwinkle appeared about to burst into tears. Her lower lip quivered and her eyes had moistened. "I get it now. You don't care about me. You got what you wanted and now you've cast me loose."

Fargo sighed.

"Your last chance," Periwinkle said. "Take me or leave me."

Fargo forked leather, the saddle creaking under him. His boots in the stirrups, he raised the reins. "Do you know why some men never get married?"

"No. Why?"

"Women like you."

Fargo tapped his spurs and left the clearing at a trot. Once in the woods he slowed. He supposed he shouldn't have said that, but she was becoming a nuisance. If she didn't control herself, she might make her parents suspicious and there would be hell to pay if the truth came out. He made a mental vow, then and there, not to ever again dally with a homesteader's daughter. But who was he kidding? he asked himself. He could no more go without that than he could go without breathing.

The tops of trees were bending to the wind. The farther he rode, the stronger the smell of smoke became.

Climbing to a prominence that would allow him a view of the mountains beyond, he passed through some firs and drew rein on an overlook.

The sight that greeted him sent a ripple of dread down his spine.

# 33

Forest fire! One of the lightning strikes was to blame. With the woods so dry, once the fire started, it rapidly spread.

Fargo beheld a quarter-mile-long front of leaping flames. Thanks to the wind, they were coming on fast. Smoke was rising, but most was dissipated by that same wind.

Fargo looked from the fire to the valley the Calloways had claimed and back to the fire again. He did some quick calculations in his head. If the wind stayed strong, the fire would reach the ridge he was on in an hour, give or take. From there it would sweep down on the Tennesseans.

They needed to be warned.

Reining around, Fargo brought the Ovaro to a trot. He hoped the wind shifted or died. If not, his friends were in for a taste of hell on earth.

Once, a few years ago, he'd come on the aftermath of a forest fire that charred hundreds of square miles of virgin wilderness. Another time, he'd been caught in a raging prairie fire and nearly lost his life.

Unlike back East, which rarely saw forest fires of any great size, the West was prone to them in the summer months. Left unchecked, some raged for days or even weeks.

The Tennesseans were in trouble if this one reached their valley. Some valleys were mostly grass, and fires could be contained better. Their valley consisted of prime timber from end to end. Stopping the flames would be impossible.

Hurrying to reach Lester's, Fargo rounded a blue spruce and had to haul on his reins.

Two men astride mounts barred his way, both pointing rifles.

Fargo was about to make a desperate draw when a mocking snarl came from his right.

"I wouldn't, were I you."

Out of the trees came Latham and Kline on horseback.

Fargo was furious at himself. In his concern for the Calloways, he'd been careless. "What the hell do you want?" he demanded.

"As if you don't know," Latham said.

"We owe you, mister," Kline said. "You have to pay for Hagler and the others. So raise those hands of yours nice and slow or die where you sit."

"If you shoot me they'll hear," Fargo stalled.

"So what?" Kline said. "It's one family. Their pa is hurt and the rest are mostly sprouts."

"Besides, we want them to hear," Latham said.

"You do?" Fargo was intent on the pair holding rifles on him. Should they let those barrels dip, he could turn the tables.

Latham gigged his horse closer. Sneering, he reached over and snatched Fargo's Colt from its holster. "Don't want you to get ideas," he said.

Fargo scowled. There was nothing he could do. If he tried to wrest the Colt back, he'd be blasted from his saddle.

"Let me show you I wasn't joshin'," Latham said. Thumbing the hammer, he pointed the Colt at the sky and fired. Not once but three times.

"What the hell?" Fargo said.

"Your homesteader friend will have heard that," Latham said. "Right about now he's hustlin' his family into their cabin. That's where they'll stay, with someone watchin' at the window for you to show up."

"Which is exactly what we want them to do," Kline said.

Fargo was confused. "What good does that do you? You can't get at them so long as they're holed up inside."

"*We* can't," Latham said.

"But somethin' else can," Kline said with a smirk.

Latham sniffed a few times. "We know about the fire. We saw it earlier, and where it's headed."

"You wouldn't," Fargo said.

"Why in hell not? They're nothin' to me. Sure, I was hankerin' to treat myself to a few of their women and however much they have in their pokes. But it's cost me too many men. Now I don't give a damn. Now I want them dead."

"But *that*," Fargo said, bobbing his head to the north. "They have kids, damn you. Their youngest isn't long out of diapers."

"As if I care."

Fargo knew that the back of the cabin faced north, and had no windows. Lester's family wouldn't realize the fire was bearing down on them until it was too late.

Latham must have been thinking the same thing. "None of them will live out the day."

"You miserable bastard."

"I'm not the one killin' them. Nature is." Latham chuckled. "With any luck, the fire will catch two or three of those backwoods bumpkins in their cabins before the rest figure out what's happenin'."

Kline laughed. "I've never seen a family burnt to death before. Not with the ma and the kids and everybody. It should be a sight."

Fargo was about to spring at Latham, but the outlaw leader suddenly pointed the Colt at him. "How about if you climb down? I've got plans for you, too."

His every impulse screaming he shouldn't, Fargo dismounted and stood with his hands high.

"Now sit," Latham commanded. "Kline, you hop to it."

The hopping consisted of Kline, grumbling because of his shoulder wound, tying Fargo's wrists and ankles and stuffing Fargo's bandanna into his mouth.

"How's that?" Kline asked.

"Perfect." Latham smiled at Fargo. "Your fangs have been pulled. All you can do is lie there when that fire comes sweepin' over the ridge."

Kline cackled. "It'll burn you to the bone, mister, and then do the same to those homesteaders in their cabin."

All four outlaws laughed.

# 34

Fargo heard the fire before he saw it.

For a seeming eternity he had been struggling against his bonds. The outlaws had ridden off, taking his guns with them. Kline had tried to take the Ovaro, but when he attempted to snag the reins, the stallion snorted and kicked and ran off. Kline was set to go after it, but Latham barked at him to forget it and get the hell out of there. The fire, Latham said, was coming on faster than they'd reckoned.

Faster than Fargo had reckoned, too. It hadn't been twenty minutes since they left, and he heard the crackling and snapping of burning timber. Worse, smoke was crawling across the ground like so much fog.

He'd managed to spit out the bandanna, but it did him little good. He was too far from Lester's cabin for them to hear if he hollered.

Fargo's only recourse was to free himself. He'd pried and pulled at his pant leg to hike it high enough to reach the Arkansas toothpick, but the rope was too tight. He'd set his fingernails to bleeding in his efforts to undo the knots.

There wasn't anything close by that could help him, either.

Desperate, he heaved to his knees and then to his feet and hopped in the direction of the cabin. Every ten feet or so he would stop and look around. He must have hopped forty yards when he spotted a rock with a jagged edge sticking out of the ground. Sitting with his back to it, he pressed the rope to the edge and rubbed as fast as he could move his arms. It seemed to take forever for the first strands to part.

Meanwhile, the fire came ever closer. So did the smoke. Borne by the wind, it crawled ahead of the flames, gray tentacles writhing and twisting as if alive.

The smoke seared his eyes and lungs and made him cough uncontrollably.

Thinking of Lester's family, Fargo rubbed with renewed vigor. He didn't care how much it hurt. He didn't care that his shoulders felt as if they were being sheared from their sockets.

The crackling and popping grew into a sustained crunching, as if a gargantuan creature were devouring the trees. It was actually wood being consumed by the fire, the same sound a campfire made, only magnified a thousand times.

The speed of the fire's advance startled him. It shouldn't, though. When conditions were right, forest fires became so hot that they incinerated everything in their path faster than a man could run or even ride.

A wall of smoke hid the bulk of the fire, but he could see flames here and there, some as high as he was tall.

Fargo couldn't imagine a worse way to die than being burned alive. The torment would be indescribable.

A whinny and the stamp of a hoof brought Fargo out of himself. The Ovaro had returned and was warily eyeing the approaching conflagration.

"Hold on, big fella," Fargo said. The moment he opened his mouth, smoke got into his lungs, provoking a fit of coughing. He considered throwing himself over his saddle with his hands still tied, but he wouldn't be able to ride as fast.

More smoke was almost on top of him. The crackling had become a roar. He was sweating profusely, and his eyes watered.

Suddenly the rope parted. With an oath of relief, Fargo attacked the one around his ankles. He couldn't undo the knots, and now fingers of flame were snaking toward him.

Fargo pushed upright, hopped to the Ovaro, and threw himself onto the saddle, belly-down. He almost fell off when the stallion shifted. Clutching the reins, he gave the Ovaro a smack and bawled, "Go!"

The stallion needed little urging. Off to the south it raced, its flaring nostrils and wide eyes showing it was more terrified of the fire than it had ever been of Apaches or wolves or ravening grizzlies.

Bouncing and flouncing, Fargo watched out for tree trunks. He couldn't control the Ovaro very well, but at least he was putting distance between them and the fire.

The roar faded and the smoke thinned and he could breathe again.

All went well until they neared the valley floor. The Ovaro veered to avoid an oak. Unprepared, Fargo felt himself roll. He caught at the saddle horn too late. His fingers slipped, and the next he knew, he was tumbling head over boots. He hit hard on his shoulders and for a few moments lay dazed, his wits in a jumble.

Tossing his head to clear it, Fargo sat up. A scritching noise high in the trees, tiny claws scraping a limb, drew his gaze to a squirrel fleeing for its life. Several does bolted by, heedless of the human in their path.

The Ovaro had stopped and was looking back.

Fargo had to free his legs. Gripping the bottom of his pant legs, he pulled with all the strength he had. His fingers were fit to break, but the rope moved a little. He stopped, gathered himself, and tried again, his teeth gritted against the pain. The rope moved a little more.

"I ever see you again, Kline, you're dead," Fargo vowed. The bastard had taken perverse delight in tying the ropes as tight as he could.

The Ovaro nickered with impatience.

"I'm trying, damn it," Fargo growled. Bunching his shoulders, he exerted every sinew.

The Ovaro nickered again, a new note to its tone. It was staring past him, its nostrils flaring.

Fargo figured the fire was to blame, even though it was a ways off. Then he looked at where the Ovaro was staring.

Another creature was fleeing the flames and coming straight toward him.

A mountain lion.

# 35

It was so unexpected Fargo turned to stone as the big cat bounded within a few yards of him. Its short ears were up; its feline eyes pierced his. For a few harrowing instants he thought the meateater would attack him, but at the last moment it swerved and sped past without so much as a glance.

"Damn," Fargo breathed. He renewed his assault on his pants. Straining for all he was worth, he succeeded in pulling the rope high enough that he could wriggle his fingers into his boot. He managed to grip the toothpick's hilt and tugged, but the knife refused to slide out.

Fargo was so mad his blood boiled hotter than the fire. He gave a powerful wrench and widened the gap enough that he could palm the toothpick. One slash was all it took. A quick cut accomplished in the blink of an eye what he hadn't been able to in long, wearying minutes of strenuous effort.

Sliding the toothpick into its sheath, Fargo jerked his pant legs down and stood. A couple of strides and he had hold of the saddle horn. Swinging up, he looked to the north.

Man-sized and larger flames leaped and danced, consuming

everything in their path. The smoke low down had mostly dissipated and now plumes and tendrils rose into the sky. Or were trying to. The wind whipped them into nothingness before they could rise very far.

Fargo rarely used his spurs hard on the Ovaro, but he used them now. Once on the valley floor he flew toward the first clearing, hoping against hope that Lester had already seen the fire and was preparing to get his family out of there before they were caught in it.

The way his luck was going, Fargo should have known that wouldn't be the case. He burst from the woods to find no one outside and the horses idling in the corral.

"Lester! Priscilla!" Fargo bellowed as he reined to a sliding halt. He was out of the saddle and reached the front door just as Lester, using his crutch, opened it.

"Land sakes," the Tennessean exclaimed. "What's all the hollerin' about?"

"You have to see for yourself." Grabbing him by the shirt, Fargo hauled him toward the side of the cabin.

Lester stumbled and nearly fell. "Hey, now!" he cried, and tried to pull free. "What's gotten into you?"

"That," Fargo said, and pointed.

Raising his head, Lester blanched. "God in heaven, no."

Pushed by the relentless wind, the fire had attained spectacular proportions. The leading front was half a mile across, a solid sheet of flame that swept the earth like a thing alive. From end to end the fire had to be a mile long, and was growing. Despite its size, not much smoke was rising. The wind again.

"Priscilla!" Lester bawled, and hobbled like mad for the front door.

His wife and the children rushed out. It didn't take long for panic to spread.

But Fargo had to hand it to them. They recovered their wits quickly and set to saddling their animals and collecting what they were going to take.

Lester discarded his crutch and used his rifle instead. He came over to where Fargo was marking the fire's progress and anxiously chewed on his bottom lip. "Do you reckon there's any chance at all that it might miss us?"

The clearing was a buffer, of sorts. The trees had been chopped down, but many of the stumps remained, and grass and weeds covered the rest. The fire might sweep to either side and spare the cabin, but Fargo wouldn't count on it, and said so.

"I was afeard as much," Lester said, choked with emotion. "Lordy, after all the work we've gone to, to lose it all."

"At least you have time to get away," Fargo said. The fire wasn't quite to the valley floor yet.

Periwinkle ran up. She had been busy helping her mother, but now she pointed and cried out, "Pa! Look yonder!"

Fargo turned, and his scalp prickled.

The inferno to the north was only part of the fire. Screened by a ridge, a spearhead of flame had swept onto the slopes on the east side of the valley and was now curling toward the valley floor.

"Dear Lord, no," Lester breathed. "It'll be here in minutes."

The family scrambled to finish saddling. All their mounts were ready and most of the children had climbed on when the mother gazed apprehensively around and said, "Where's Beaumont?"

Lester, cramming a saddlebag with jerky, replied, "He was here a minute or two ago."

"No, Pa," Periwinkle said. "I haven't seen him in a good long while. Not since Skye showed up."

Lester glared about the clearing and cupped a hand to his mouth. "Beaumont? Where in tarnation are you?"

There was no answer.

The mother rushed inside and wasn't in there a minute when she came back out worriedly shaking her head. "He's not in there, either."

"What the hell?" Lester said.

"Don't cuss in front of the children," Priscilla scolded. "You know how I feel about that."

"You fret about language at a time like this?" Lester said. "But forget it. Where the blazes is that boy?"

"I'll look for him," Fargo offered, and hurried to the Ovaro. Trotting to the edge of the woods, he saw no sign of him.

The flames weren't a hundred yards away, rushing like runners eager to reach the finish line.

"Beaumont?" Fargo called out. "Are you in there?"

His answer was a scream of terror.

"Help me! Help me! I'm caught!"

The cry came from Fargo's left. He entered the woods and was immediately in a particulate mist that burned his eyes and made him hold his breath. Squinting, he scoured the under-growth. "Where are you?"

"Here! Over here!"

Fargo's blood turned to ice in his veins.

An oak had fallen, pinning Beaumont's legs. Not only that, but the tree was partly aflame. Coughing violently, tears streaking his face, Beaumont was frenziedly trying to free himself. "Help me!" he wailed anew.

Not thirty yards from the oak raged the leading line of the fire.

Vaulting down, Fargo sprinted to the boy's aid. The heat was blistering, the air so hot he could scarcely stand to breathe. He reached the oak, bent, and lifted. The trunk refused to budge.

"Get me out!" Beaumont shrieked.

Fargo firmed his hold and tried again.

"I just wanted a look at the fire," the boy blubbered. "And this darned tree fell on me."

Fargo didn't waste breath telling the boy it was a damn stupid thing to do. Girding his legs, he tried again.

A branch, snagged on another tree, thwarted him.

"What are you waitin' for?" Beaumont yelled, squirming furiously. "I'm burnin'! I'm burnin'!"

No, the boy wasn't. But he would be soon unless Fargo did something. Darting to the branch that was stuck, he kicked it, attempting to free it so he could lift the oak. He kicked again and again, and just when part of it snapped off, the boy screeched his name.

"Look out! Behind you!"

Fargo whirled.

Another tree was falling—on top of him.

# 36

The tree was another oak, the upper branches crackling with fire.

Fargo took a long bound and leaped. Diving and rolling, he felt a jolt on his shoulder and a burning pain on his neck. A branch had clipped him as the tree came down, and a spark or cinder had sizzled on his skin.

The tree barely missed Beaumont, who was bucking and pushing in a paroxysm of fear.

Springing to the tree that had the boy trapped, Fargo tried again to raise it. This time he succeeded.

Beaumont scrambled out from under and went to stand, but his leg buckled and he let out a bleat of agony.

Fargo reached him before he fell and scooped the boy into his arms. Instead of being grateful, Beaumont pushed at his chest.

"Let me go! Let me go!"

Fargo had had enough. "Stop your squalling," he snapped, and shook the boy, hard.

The fire was much too close.

The roar in his ears, volcanic wind-spawned breath on the back of his neck, Fargo sprinted to the Ovaro. He practically threw the boy on, shouting, "Grab the horn!" Springing up, he reined around and raced for the clearing.

Lester and Periwinkle were on their horses, rushing to help, but stopped when they saw he had the boy.

"Get the hell out of here!" Fargo yelled. Galloping past them, he rode to where Priscilla was standing with the other children, gripped Beaumont by the wrist, and swung him into her arms.

Hugging him, Priscilla closed her eyes. "Thank you, thank you, thank you," she exclaimed.

"No time for that," Fargo said. "Light a shuck."

The prong of fire to the east had reached the clearing. Almost immediately the grass caught.

"Go! Go!" Lester cried to his loved ones. "Head for the next cabin and don't stop for anything."

The children obeyed. The mother got Beaumont on his horse and clambered onto her own, and the pair raced off.

Lester was staring forlornly at his cabin and the burning grass that licked toward it. "This can't be happenin'! We'll lose most everything."

Periwinkle slapped his horse on the rump. "Ride, Pa, ride!" She followed right behind, her body a bow.

Fargo brought up the rear. His last glance at their cabin showed tongues of flames climbing the east wall and fiery meteors blazing down from the surrounding trees.

Once they'd put some distance behind them, he breathed a little easier.

Lester caught up to his wife and their kids. Both he and his missus were trying hard not to show their despair.

Periwinkle didn't seem the least bit concerned. Slowing so that she could ride alongside the Ovaro, she remarked, "That was harrowing."

"You don't appear very frazzled," Fargo said.

"We're alive, aren't we?" she replied. "Thank you for savin' my lunkhead of a brother, by the way. He shouldn't ought to have strayed off like he did." She looked back. "It puts a crimp in things, this fire. I had plans for you and me for tonight and now we won't be able to."

"Is that all you can think of?" Fargo would have thought she'd be more upset about their home burning to the ground.

"I'm sad to say it is," Periwinkle said. "You have yourself to blame. Until you came along, I hardly ever thought about it. But ever since you had your way with me, it's all I have on my mind."

"The urge will go away," Fargo assured her, even though his own never had. If anything, his craving for women was stronger than ever.

"I hope not," Periwinkle said. "You stoked somethin' in me that was buried deep, somethin' I'd been hidin' even from myself."

"That you like men?"

Periwinkle blushed. "That I like the feelin's you brought out of me. The pleasure when I let myself go."

"Imagine that," Fargo said dryly.

"I hope we can do it again real soon," Periwinkle said, and held up her hand when he went to reply. "I know what you're goin' to say. But I truly can't help myself. You've kindled a fire in me as hot as the one off in those woods, and the only one who can put it out is you." She smiled and tapped her heels and rode on ahead.

"Wonderful," Fargo muttered.

He held the Ovaro to a fast walk. The stallion was already lathered from the hard riding he'd been doing, and so long as they stayed ahead of the blaze, they weren't in any danger.

Suddenly the underbrush crashed to the passage of a large animal. A buck hurtled into the clear, saw Fargo and snorted at him, and plunged on.

Birds were next, a flock of sparrows that flapped past as if they couldn't fly fast enough.

Fargo saw a gray squirrel seek shelter in its nest high in a tree. If it stayed there it would be burned to a cinder. It made him think of how many other animals would perish, and what would happen if a Flathead hunting party were caught in the fire's path. That, in turn, made him think of the cavalry patrol. By now Captain Benson must be fit to be tied. Fargo should have reported back the day before, but if he had, he wouldn't have seen the fire and warned Lester and his family, and they might now be dead.

Deep in thought, Fargo didn't realize something new was bearing down on him until he heard the thud of heavy footfalls. Twisting in the saddle, he beheld a large black bear. He figured it was the she-bear from before but didn't see a cub. Then it hit him. This was another bear entirely.

A bear that spread its maw and roared.

# 37

Fargo reined aside, thinking the black bear would run past. To his consternation, the bear slowed, its eyes fastened on the Ovaro. Fargo's hand was on his Colt, and when the bear abruptly started to rear, he drew and thumbed a shot into the ground in front of it.

Black bears weren't grizzlies; they were more timid. A gunshot would often scare one off.

Not this one. The bear rose onto its hind legs and gaped its teeth wide while growling deep in its barrel chest.

"Damn it, go!" Fargo shouted.

Before he could shoot again, the Ovaro acted on its own accord. Whinnying, the stallion reared and flailed at the black bear with its front hooves. The heavy thuds reminded Fargo of sledgehammer blows.

The black bear was knocked back, stumbled, and fell. It tried to rise, but the Ovaro wasn't done. A front hoof caught the bear on the shoulder and sent it sprawling.

Where a grizzly would have been incensed and gone berserk, the black bear scrambled up, bawled like a cub, and fled.

The Ovaro snorted and stamped and let it go.

"I reckon you taught him," Fargo said, patting the stallion's neck.

As soon as the bear was out of sight, he reloaded and rode to overtake Lester's family. They were well ahead, and he had to gallop. He didn't overtake them until he reached the next clearing.

It was Solomon's, and he and his family were scurrying to get ready to leave.

"We only saw the smoke a while ago," Solomon related as Fargo dismounted. "I was fixin' to come warn Lester when he came ridin' out of the woods to warn us."

While Solomon and his family saddled the last of their horses, Fargo kept an eye on the forest fire. Thick columns of smoke rose to the north, enough to blot out part of the sky. Smoke also rose from the slopes to the east, where the fire appeared to be moving faster. A freak of the wind, Fargo reckoned, even as a strong gust fanned his face. He looked to the west but saw no evidence of fire on the facing slopes. The way to the south was still clear, too.

They got under way. Once again Fargo rode last, and once again he acquired a partner.

"Well, that's it, then," Periwinkle said forlornly.

"I must have missed what that is," Fargo said.

Periwinkle looked as if she might cry. "I'm talkin' about you and me havin' a chance to do it."

"Not again," Fargo said.

"Once all the families are together, we won't have any privacy," Periwinkle said sadly. "There will be kids everywhere, and the parents, besides."

Fargo would have laughed at her theatrics, but she might be offended. Instead he said, "You never know."

Periwinkle brightened. "I thank you for that."

"For what?"

"Showin' you do want to, after all. I was commencin' to think you didn't want me anymore, but now I see you haven't given up hope. That means a lot."

"I'm happy to hear it," Fargo growled.

"Maybe we'll have a chance tonight," Periwinkle said hopefully. "We'll have picked up Uncle Rufus and his family, and Uncle Vernon and his, and will be at Uncle Granville's by sundown. I wonder if we'll stay there for the night."

"It depends on the fire," Fargo said. If the wind died, there was no hurry. If not, the fire might reach the end of the valley before the night was out.

"They'll likely hold a family meetin' and decide whether to stay or go," Periwinkle said. "If all of us lose our cabins—" She stopped and swallowed. "I'd rather not think about that. It would be a calamity."

"You can always rebuild," Fargo said. "There's plenty of time before the cold weather hits."

"Maybe so. But it could be an omen this ain't the right place for us."

"There's no such thing," Fargo said.

"As an omen?" Periwinkle was shocked. "Why, sure there is. Everybody knows that. Back to home, the soothsayers were always readin' omens in tea leaves and cards and such."

"If you say so."

"I had a powerful omen my own self the first time I set eyes on you. It's why I decided to let you be my first."

"*You* had an omen?" Fargo said in surprise. "What was it?"

"The way you looked at me. Like you were a wolf and I was a lamb you hankered to eat."

"That was your omen?"

"What would you call it?"

"Being male."

Periwinkle laughed. "I never know when you're serious."

Fargo was spared further silliness by Lester and Solomon riding back up the line and swinging in on his other side.

"We have a problem," Lester announced.

"And we don't mean the fire," Solomon said.

"I'm listening," Fargo said.

"My missus says she spotted someone off in the trees to the west watchin' us," Lester reported.

"A Flathead?"

"No. It weren't no Injun," Lester said. "From how she described him, I think it was that no-account killer, Latham."

"That is a problem," Fargo agreed.

"One of us needs to go have a look-see," Lester proposed. "If you'll keep watch on things, it'll be me."

"I can do it," Solomon said.

"You both have families," Fargo said, and breaking away, he headed west.

"Be careful," Periwinkle hollered after him. "We wouldn't want anything to happen to you."

Fargo wondered what Latham was up to now. Were the outlaws shadowing them, or was there something more sinister involved? He regretted more than ever not contacting the patrol. The settlers would have a cavalry escort by now, and the outlaws would have no choice but to light out for safer pastures.

Smoke blown ahead of the fire hung in the air. Here and there tendrils writhed, and now and then a spark fell from the sky. Those embers were cause for concern. Should one fall on some dry leaves, the leaves might ignite and a new fire would soon be raging through the woods.

The wildlife was still fleeing. Several deer ran past, a sizable buck among them.

Out of nowhere a cow elk and her calf trotted by. Fargo glimpsed a normally elusive fox that paused to stare. Birds winged overhead in increasing numbers, robins and grosbeaks and more.

Just ahead the valley floor ended and the slope of a mountain rose thick with timber. If the outlaws were up there, ferreting them out would take a while.

Fargo drew rein to scan the forest—and a shot boomed.

# 38

Fargo was turning his head to look to the north. The movement saved his life. The slug buzzed his ear instead of coring his skull, and the next moment he had reined around and was flying toward a stand of saplings. He made it without another shot being fired.

Swinging off, Fargo shucked the Henry and stalked to where he could see the slope. He had a fair idea where the shot came from. Whoever it was had gone to ground.

That there had only been the one shot puzzled him. Four outlaws were still alive. A volley would have blasted him from the saddle.

It could be, he told himself, that only one of them was keeping an eye on the settlers.

Fargo stayed still, waiting for the shooter to reveal himself. Smoke continued to drift in, though, lending the mountain a hazy aspect and making it harder to see.

He was debating how long to stay there when something moved. The impression he had was of a man in a crouch, climbing. About thirty feet higher was a small open space. He imagined the outlaw would be savvy enough to avoid it, but you never knew. Pressing the Henry to his shoulder, he drew back the hammer and sighted on the clear space.

The seconds dragged. Suddenly a squat shape in a high-crowned hat was in Fargo's sights. Instantly he fired.

Up on the mountain, the shooter cried out and seemed to flop into cover.

Fargo worked the Henry's lever and had to flatten as the man up above sprayed lead in his direction. The shooter didn't know exactly where he was, but some of the shots came too close for comfort.

Fargo looked for telltale puffs of gun smoke, but with so much smoke from the fire, he couldn't spot any.

Flattening, he crawled to a different position, prudently keeping trees between him and where he believed the shooter to be. He came to a blue spruce and started to rise, then had to flatten again as the man on the mountain cut loose with half a dozen shots that clipped needles and small branches. Rolling, Fargo ran to a pine with a wide trunk. Lead thwacked the other side, and the firing stopped.

To the north a heavy bank of smoke crept toward him. To the east, but farther away, was more.

Fargo poked his head out and snapped a shot to see what would happen. The shooter didn't take the bait. Darting to another tree, Fargo braced for more blasts. Again, nothing happened.

The fact that he hadn't heard the drum of hoofbeats told Fargo the man must still be up there. Fargo could always sneak to the Ovaro and ride off, but then he'd have the outlaw at his back.

Tucking at the waist, Fargo dashed to a ponderosa. Lead kicked up dirt at his feet. He made it and put his back to the bole.

Some time ago, Fargo had come across a newspaper account where a journalist described a shooting affray between a pair of gamblers as a pistol duel. What he had here was a rifle duel.

Again Fargo broke for a different tree. Again the shooter on the mountain tried to bring him down. Fargo returned fire as he ran and must have come close because a yelp greeted his last shot.

With a new tree to his back, Fargo fished in his pocket and replaced the spent cartridges. As he did, he heard, faintly, the ratchet of a lever. The outlaw was doing the same.

Fargo smothered a cough. The smoke was becoming worse. That thick bank wasn't more than fifty yards away. And the wind was as strong as ever, if not stronger.

Ducking, Fargo weaved toward a boulder. He was almost to it when a slug sent chips flying. One stung his cheek. Hunkering, he touched the spot and had blood on his finger.

Taking off his hat, Fargo threw it to the right and poked around the boulder to the left. The outlaw fired at his hat. He fired at the outlaw.

Drawing back, Fargo hooked the hat with his Henry and pulled it near enough to grab it and jam it on.

Up on the mountain, the outlaw was cussing.

Gauging the distance to a nearby tree, Fargo crabbed toward it as if his pants were on fire. He heard another, louder curse and the bang of the shooter's rifle. Dirt erupted, catching him in the eye. Blinking to clear it, he gained the cover of the tree.

His eyes began to water. Not from the dirt, but from the

smoke. Swiping with a sleeve, Fargo took stock of the situation. Sooner or later the outlaw would wise up and anticipate what his next move would be, just as he had done when the man crossed that clear space a while ago.

At the moment, he could break right or left. That's what the outlaw expected.

Fargo decided to do something different. Keeping his arms to his sides so he didn't show himself, he slowly unfolded to his full height. Turning, he removed his hat and inched an eye far enough to see the slope.

The smoke was a gray smog that hid patches of the forest. But it didn't hide the spot where Fargo believed the outlaw to be.

Easing the Henry up, Fargo slid it across a low branch. He put his cheek to the brass receiver, cocked the hammer, and curled his finger to the trigger. Then, without moving his head, he gave voice to a hostile war whoop. He'd heard them enough times, when set upon by the Sioux and the Blackfeet and others, that his was convincing.

A head appeared, looking every which way.

*Got you,* Fargo thought, and fired.

In a splash of red the head vanished and a bush shook to violent thrashing.

Springing from concealment, Fargo hurtled up the slope. The bush was still thrashing when he reached it. Leveling the Henry, he charged around.

The slug had ripped through the outlaw's neck and he'd bled like a stuck pig. Still alive, he was opening and closing his mouth spasmodically. The man tried to rise onto his elbows when Fargo appeared, but he was too weak. His eyes were pools of hate.

"You've killed me, you son of a bitch."

"Don't expect tears," Fargo said as he moved to the man's rifle and kicked it out of reach.

The outlaw coughed, blood dribbling from both corners of his mouth. "All I was supposed to do was keep an eye on those hill folk."

"Then you shouldn't have shot at me."

"I saw a chance and I took it." The man did more coughing. "I'd've had you, too, but you're so damn quick."

"Do you have a handle?" Fargo asked. "Or do I just tell Latham I killed the stupid one?"

"Go to hell. He'll get you in the end. When Latham sets his mind to stomethin', there's no stoppin' him."

"If he's smart he'll ride and forget all this."

"Not Latham," the man said. "You don't know him like I do. Once he sets his mind to somethin', he does it or dies tryin'."

"It's just as well," Fargo said.

The man's voice had been growing weaker by the moment, and now he could barely whisper as he said, "How do you figure?"

"Latham isn't leaving these mountains alive."

"Big talk," the outlaw scoffed. "He's made coyote bait of tougher hombres than you." The man closed his eyes and groaned. "My head is spinnin'. Do me a favor and put me out of my misery."

"No."

The outlaw looked at him. "I'd do it for you if it was me holdin' that rifle and you who was shot."

"Only it's not."

The man muttered something, then said, "You have a lot of hard bark on you, mister. But so does Latham. He's killed pretty near twenty that I know about, not countin' women and Mexicans."

"Is that all?"

"You'll be laughin' out the other side of your ass before Latham is done. I wouldn't want to be you for all the gold there was."

"Are you going to die or talk me to death?"

The outlaw swore, convulsed, and died.

"That leaves three of you," Fargo said to the corpse. He squatted to search the body but jumped up at a whinny from the Ovaro. Smoke blocked his view of the saplings, but he didn't need to see them to realize the peril the stallion was in.

Sheets of flame were advancing on the stand with harrowing speed.

The forest fire had caught up to them.

# 39

Fargo flew down the slope on wings of fear. He'd wrapped the Ovaro's reins around one of the trees, and from the Ovaro's strident whinnies and the shaking of the saplings, he could tell the stallion was trying to pull free and flee.

Fargo reached the bottom, and his fear worsened. A break in the smoke revealed a crackling wall of fire so close to the saplings it was a wonder the heat alone hadn't sent the stallion to its knees. He willed his legs to pump faster, but he was already flat out.

Then there came the loudest whinny yet and the Ovaro exploded out of the saplings, the reins dangling. Head high, mane flying, the stallion galloped madly to the south.

Fargo shouted for it to stop, but either the Ovaro didn't hear him or the stallion was too panicked.

Suddenly Fargo was confronted with a dire problem. He was stranded afoot, and the fire was almost to him.

He ran for his life.

The roar grew louder in his ears. The crackling and rending made it sound as if a giant were smashing the trees to bits.

Fargo glanced over his shoulder, and swallowed. The furnace of flame was overtaking him. The nearest were mere yards from his boot heels, the flames so bright it hurt to look into them, the heat withering in its intensity.

Fargo's chest began to hurt. But he ran on. His legs protested with spikes of pain. But he ran on. To stop was to die, and Fargo was fond of living. Some people might throw up their hands in resignation and give up, but not him. Never him. Giving up wasn't in his nature. He would fight tenaciously for his life, and if he did go down, he'd die knowing he'd tried his utmost.

The smoke made it increasingly difficult to breathe. Gray snakes enfolded him and clung as if to prevent him from getting away. He tried to suck in a breath without getting any smoke in his lungs, and a fit of coughing seized him. His eyes stung fiercely. He blinked to clear them, but it was like looking through water at the bottom of a lake.

He realized almost too late that something large and alive was in his path, and barely had time to dig his heels in and come to a sliding stop. For a few harrowing heartbeats he thought it was the black bear that had attacked him earlier.

His vision cleared, and he cried out in relief.

It was the Ovaro. The stallion had stopped to wait for him. In a bound he was in the saddle and lashing the reins.

When next Fargo looked back, he had put the fire a fair distance behind him. He still had smoke in his lungs and couldn't stop coughing, and his eyes burned, but he was alive, by God.

The tops of the trees were bending to the wind. That was the real danger. The damnable wind. If it would die, the fire would stall. If only.

Fargo rode until he reached the next clearing. It was Rufus's place, and Fargo was taken aback to see the corral was empty and no one anywhere around.

Then Periwinkle came around the cabin on her horse and drew rein. "You made it!" she exclaimed happily. "I was gettin' worried."

Fargo coughed, and motioned. "Where is everyone?"

"Rufus's missus was too scared to wait. She was pretty near hysterical, so Pa and the other men decided to push on to Vernon's. Pa said it was all right for me to stay and make sure you got here." Periwinkle unslung a canteen from her saddle horn and held it out. "You look like you could use this."

"Could I ever!" Fargo admitted. He swallowed greedily. The water soothed the irritation in his throat and stopped his coughing.

"Will you look at that?" Periwinkle said, gazing northward. "It must be what Hades looks like."

To the north and east, the woods were orange and red for as far as the eye could see, an ocean of writhing, rapidly multiplying flames.

Capping the canteen, Fargo handed it back. As he did he happened to glance to the west and thought he spied wisps of smoke rising from a ridge. He waited to see if more rose, but none did.

"Somethin' the matter?"

"Guess not," Fargo said. "Let's ride."

They held to a trot until they were halfway to the next clearing, at which point Fargo slowed to spare the Ovaro.

"Isn't this nice?" Periwinkle said, riding at his side.

"What is?"

"You and me, together," she said. "It's like God is tryin' to tell us somethin'."

Fargo couldn't believe it. Here her family had lost their home and they were running for their lives with a forest fire and outlaws to worry about, and all she cared about was being with him. "You're loco, girl."

"I ain't, neither," Periwinkle said. "Why would you say such a thing? I can't help how I feel about you."

"Don't start with that again."

"I know, I know," Periwinkle said. "You're goin' to say it's not the right time or place. And I agree."

"You do?" Fargo said suspiciously.

"I'm not plumb stupid," Periwinkle said. "When this is over with, that's when we'll hash this out."

"Hash what out?"

"Why, you and me, of course. As man and wife. If you were to ask me, I'd say yes before the words were out of your mouth."

"I thought we had that all worked out," Fargo reminded her. "I never said anything about marrying you." He had to get it through her head that wasn't going to happen.

"After what we did, that's only natural, ain't it? Back to home, it was proof a fella's intentions were true."

"Damn it all," Fargo said, angry now. "I thought all you wanted was to make love."

"That, too."

Fargo tried mentally counting to ten. It didn't work. "Let's get one thing plain here and now. I'm not looking for a wife."

"A woman gives her body to you, that should count for somethin.'"

"Don't you dare."

"I'll do as I please, thank you," Periwinkle declared. "I've thought about it and thought about it and changed my mind again. It would please me very much to have you as my husband. For now, we have the stupid fire to deal with, but once we're in the clear and everyone is safe, I'll ask Pa to call a family meetin'."

"Do what?"

"I'll tell everyone how you had your way with me. They'll

agree it's proper and fittin' that you do right and take my hand in wedlock."

"You wouldn't," Fargo said, knowing full well she would.

"I'd rather you come right out and ask me. But since you're not goin' to, we'll do it the hard way. And back in the hills, the hard way is for the girl's pa to escort the groom to the altar at the business end of a shotgun."

Fargo was furious. As if he didn't have enough trouble to deal with.

"Now, now." Periwinkle smiled sweetly. "I can understand you bein' in a huff, but that will change. Once we're man and wife, you'll thank me. Just wait and see if you don't."

# 40

The clearing around Vernon's cabin was filled with horses and kids too frightened to scamper about. The adults were clustered together talking.

"We were waitin' for you two," Lester said as Fargo and Periwinkle rode up. "What in tarnation kept you?"

Fargo half dreaded Periwinkle would bring up the marrying business, so he quickly related his run-in with the outlaw.

"There're only three of them now," Rufus said. "If'n they have any brains, they'll light a shuck while they can."

"With all of us together now, they won't dare show themselves," Vernon said. "Our worry is that fire. I hate losin' my cabin."

"You think I didn't?" Lester said.

"Or me?" Solomon said.

"We can rebuild," Rufus said. "By winter we'll be snug as bugs in a rug."

"Most of the forest will be gone," Vernon said.

Rufus bobbed his head to the west. "There's still plenty of timber yonder. We can chop down the trees and haul them."

That reminded Fargo. He turned and scoured the western slopes for sign of smoke but didn't spot any.

"We'd best be movin' on to Granville's," Solomon suggested. "That wind will have the fire here in no time."

"I'll ride on ahead," Fargo offered. "Keep an eye out for Latham." His real reason was to be shed of his would-be betrothed.

"I'll go with you," Periwinkle said.

"Like blazes you will," Lester said. "You'll stay with your ma and me and help us with the young'uns."

"But, Pa, him and me—"

Lester held up a hand. "No sass, you hear? A time like this, a family's got to stick together."

Fargo could have hugged him. He smiled at Periwinkle and was under way before she could raise a fuss. Once the clearing was behind him, he chuckled and came to a trot. It wasn't far to Granville's, about a quarter of a mile, and before long the clearing came into view. The horses were in the corral and there was no sign of the family. That puzzled him. They were bound to have seen the smoke by now.

Drawing rein at the edge of the trees, Fargo shucked the Henry. Something wasn't right. He reached the front of the cabin, threw himself from the saddle, and hit the front door at a run with his shoulder. It flew inward and he spilled to a knee, leveling his rifle as he fell.

"What in the world?" Charlotte Calloway exclaimed. She was standing at the head of the table, holding a book. Her kids, Darlene included, were either seated around it or cross-legged on the floor.

Granville was over by the fireplace, honing a knife. "You could have just knocked," he said, and laughed.

So did some of the kids.

Lowering the Henry, Fargo pushed to his feet. "What are you doing?" he asked in amazement.

"What does it look like?" Charlotte replied. "The children are havin' their schoolin'. Three times a week we devote a couple of hours to readin' and writin' and arithmetic. Just like we did back to Tennessee."

Granville nodded. "She's a stickler for it. I've always told her she'd make a fine schoolmarm, but she says she couldn't do that and raise a family both, and her family is more important."

"Your schooling is over for a while," Fargo said.

"I beg your pardon?" Charlotte said.

"I could tell you, but come out and see for yourselves."

The kids chattered as their parents ushered them outside. One look was enough to cause shocked silence.

The north half of the valley and the slopes to the east were nothing but flames spewing smoke in thick plumes.

"Dear Lord!" Charlotte gasped.

Granville moved in a daze past the others, his gaze riveted to the wildfire. "The lightning, you reckon?"

"That would be my guess," Fargo said.

"Not those outlaws?"

Fargo hadn't thought of that. He wouldn't put it past Latham to get revenge on the Tennesseans by burning them out. "I saw a few strikes last night."

Granville gave a start. "Lester's place? Solomon's?"

"Gone," Fargo said. "But your brothers are safe and on their way here. I came on ahead."

Charlotte broke the spell of horrid fascination by turning to her kids and loudly clapping her hands to get their attention. "Everyone, listen up. We don't have a lot of time. We need the animals saddled, the packhorses readied. You have to collect whatever you want to take."

"I'll see to the horses," Darlene volunteered. "Miranda and Zeke can lend me a hand."

"Off you go," Charlotte said. "No dawdlin', you hear?"

Granville looked sorrowfully at Fargo. "All our cabins. All we've done since we got here. It will all have been for nothin'."

Fargo didn't reply.

"We made it all this way. We've worked so hard. . . ." Granville stopped and raised his face to the smoke-filled sky. "Why, Lord? Why?"

"You don't have a lot of time," Fargo mentioned.

"We'd have even less if you hadn't come to warn us," Granville said. "I'm grateful." He put his hand on Fargo's shoulder, then hurried inside.

Fargo walked around the cabin to the corral. Darlene and her sister and brother had opened the gate and were throwing saddle blankets and saddles on the family's mounts.

Darlene saw him and said without stopping, "Nice to see you in one piece. I was worried those outlaws might have done you in."

"They're trying," Fargo said, and gestured at the animals. "Tell me which saddle to throw on which horse and I'll help."

126

"You can help more by takin' the ones we saddle out and tyin' them to the rails so everybody can get to them quick when we go to leave."

Fargo took the reins to a horse her sister had just saddled and the reins to a sorrel her brother had finished with and led them out the gate. He saw no sign of Lester and Rufus and the rest, but the others should be there soon.

Darlene had a horse ready for him when he went back in. As she passed the reins over, she asked, "How have you and Periwinkle been gettin' along?"

"Why bring her up?" Fargo said testily. He didn't care to be reminded of her antics.

"I saw how she was lookin' at you after the dance. Seems to me that my cousin is mighty smitten."

"Your cousin has rocks for brains."

Darlene laughed but caught herself and stared to the west with her eyebrows trying to climb up into her hair. "Oh no. Is that what I think it is?"

Fargo spun.

Through a gap in the wooded slopes to the west, a new river of searing flame was flowing.

# 41

Now Fargo knew the cause of the smoke he'd seen earlier. Just as the wind had driven the fire onto the slopes on the east side of the valley, it had done the same to the west. Only instead of sweeping along the facing slopes, the fire had pushed behind them and now had funneled through that gap and was spreading outward, toward the valley and toward them.

Darlene clasped a hand on her throat. "We'll be trapped if that fire reaches us before we can leave."

"Keep saddling," Fargo said, and ran around to the front door.

Granville and Charlotte and some of their kids were scurrying madly about and cramming things into packs. Granville glanced up, his face a question mark.

"You need to see," Fargo said.

"Not again. What is it now?"

Everyone rushed outside. The horror of it rooted them, until one of the younger girls let out a wail of despair.

"Tamara, control yourself," Charlotte chided. "Get back inside and keep on packin'. All of you."

"That fire is comin' on fast," Granville said, and gazed to the north. "Will the others get here before it does?"

"I can go hurry them," Fargo offered.

"I'd be obliged," Granville said, and then, under his breath, more to himself than to Fargo, he said, "God help us."

Fargo ran to the Ovaro. No sooner did he leave the clearing than the smoke became as thick as fog. Visibility was slashed to ten to twenty feet. He didn't dare go faster than a trot or he invited calamity. Breathing became torment. Stopping, he untied his bandanna, placed it over his mouth and nose, retied it, and rode on.

The soup would slow the others. It would also prevent them from seeing the new threat to the west.

Suddenly a four-legged form flashed out of the murk. A buck, terror-stricken, nearly collided with the Ovaro. At the last moment it leaped aside.

Impossibly, the smoke became thicker. Fargo couldn't see more than the length of the Ovaro. Rising in the stirrups, he lifted his bandanna from his mouth. "Lester! Rufus! Vernon! Can you hear me?"

There was no answer.

At half-minute intervals Fargo shouted again. The third time, he thought he heard a faint holler. He rode faster and kept on shouting. He was answered from off to the west. It sounded like Vernon.

"Here! We're over here!"

Even with the bandanna, Fargo found it hard to breathe. He had to take shallow breaths and held them before taking another.

The Ovaro was in respiratory distress, too, with a lot of snorts and heavy breaths and shakings of its head.

Figures appeared in the gloom. The Tennesseans were huddled together, moving as slowly as turtles, groping their way. Many were coughing and had their hands over their mouths and noses, or had done as Fargo did and used a bandanna or a scarf. Cries of relief were raised when they spotted him.

"Are we glad to see you!" Lester exclaimed, limping up as Fargo drew rein.

"This damn smoke," Rufus said. "We're not sure we're headed in the right direction."

"You are," Fargo confirmed, "but you've drifted to the west." He quickly told them about the new arm of the fire, ending with "We have to get you out of here or you'll be cut off."

"We don't want that," Solomon said.

"Lead the way," Vernon said.

From his vantage on his saddle, Fargo looked out over the others. "You haven't lost anyone?"

"Not that we know of," Rufus said.

"Periwinkle's safe, ain't she?" Lester asked.

"Periwinkle?" Fargo said.

"She rode on after you not long after you lit out," Lester said. "Told us it was important she talk to you."

"About what?"

"She wouldn't say," Lester said. "But she made such a fuss, her ma and me let her go." He paused. "Are you sayin' you haven't seen her?"

"Not since I left you."

"Oh God," Lester said, and peered anxiously into the smoke. "She must have got turned around."

"Don't worry," Rufus said. "If she's not at Granville's when we get there, we'll fire shots into the air. That will help her find us, easy."

Fargo refrained from mentioning that they might not have the time. The fire from the west was coming fast. "We have to hurry."

"Then let's get crackin'," Lester said.

Fargo led. Long ago he'd discovered that he had a knack—some would call it a gift—for telling east from west and north from south, even without landmarks. A professor he'd once guided into the Rockies to collect specimens called it an "innate ability," whatever that meant. It served him in good stead now. He soon had the Tennesseans moving down the middle of the valley at a much faster pace than before.

Still, it was hell. The smoke was atrocious. Some of the kids couldn't take it and had to be helped along, hacking and crying.

The smoke was so thick that Fargo had emerged from the woods and was well into Granville's clearing before he realized it. "We're here!" he bellowed. "Get to the cabin, quick."

Granville and Charlotte were waiting. All their mounts were

saddled and their pack animals laden with possessions. The kids were all on their horses except for Darlene.

Fargo sought sign of the fire to the west, but he couldn't see the edge of the clearing, let alone the forest beyond.

He heard his name, and turned.

"It's Periwinkle," Lester said, unable to hide his fear. "Granville says she never showed up."

The oldest brother shook his head. "We never saw hide nor hair of her. She must be out there lost."

"Lord help us," Lester's wife, Priscilla, mewed, and burst into tears. Charlotte hugged her to comfort her.

"We should go look," Granville proposed. "Spread out so we can cover more ground."

"And wind up as lost as she is?" Fargo said. "Besides, you don't know how close the fire is."

"We can't just leave her," Rufus said. "The Calloways don't ever desert one of their own."

"How about if I get all of you out of here and come back for her once you're safe?" Fargo said.

"I'm not goin' anywhere without my girl," Lester declared.

"Me, either," the mother said between sobs.

A discussion broke out over who should go look and who should stay.

Fargo shook his head with impatience. They didn't have time for this. None of them seemed aware of the danger they were in.

Then a girl of ten or so pointed to the west and screamed.

# 42

They had run out of time.

Great sheets of sizzling flame were rushing toward the clearing from the west. The line stretched to the north as far as the smoke allowed them to see.

"God in heaven!" one of the wives wailed.

Granville's face was slack with dismay. "No," he said bleakly. "Not now. We have to find Periwinkle."

Fargo grabbed him by the front of his shirt and shook him. "Snap out of it! Can you find your way out on your own?"

Granville blinked, and nodded. "It shouldn't be hard. We're near the mouth of the valley. If we can beat that fire—" He didn't finish.

"Then you take them," Fargo said. "I'll go back for Periwinkle." It was the only way he could think of to get them out of there before it was too late.

"She's our'n," Lester said. "I'm goin' with you."

"Me, too," Rufus said.

"No, you're not," Fargo said. "Your families will need all the help you can give them." He almost added, "To make it out alive."

"He's right." Granville ended the debate. "We're all leavin', right this minute." He gripped Fargo's arm. "Find that poor girl."

"I'll try my best." Fargo turned to climb onto the Ovaro.

"And, mister?" Granville said.

Fargo looked at him.

"We can't ever thank you enough for all you've done. I mean that from the bottom of my heart."

"Get the hell out of here," Fargo said, and smiled. He didn't waste another moment but swung onto the Ovaro and headed back around the corral. His last glimpse of the Tennesseans was the fathers and mothers hustling their broods away.

His eyes smarting fiercely, Fargo entered the woods. To the west the roaring wall of flame was perilously near. He shouted Periwinkle's name over and over. Each time he did, the smoke seared his throat. At times he could scarcely breathe.

Fargo figured that Periwinkle had lost her way and drifted toward the east side of the valley. Had she drifted to the west, she would have heard all the yells earlier and shouted to get their attention.

The undergrowth rustled and out of it loped a wolf. Its hair was singed and giving off smoke. Startled by the Ovaro, it stopped and crouched and snarled.

"Keep going," Fargo said, his hand on his Colt. "You have bigger worries than us."

The wolf pricked its ears and quizzically tilted its gray head, then uttered a sharp bark and raced away.

"Wish I was going with you," Fargo said under his breath. He resumed shouting for Periwinkle.

There was no response.

Fargo wondered if she had gotten so lost in the smoke that she had inadvertently turned around and gone back the way she came. He reasoned she was bound to have realized her mistake once she saw the main body of the fire, so he kept to the east.

The smoke was almost unbearable. He couldn't see his hand at arm's length. Enough was enough, he told himself, and drew rein. He'd done all he could. If he didn't get out of there, he and the Ovaro might be trapped. He yelled one last time and went to rein around.

"Help me!"

The cry was so weak Fargo couldn't tell where it came from. "Periwinkle! Where are you?"

"Here!" was her reply. "Help me!"

"Keep hollering so I can find you!" Fargo shouted. He still couldn't tell where she was.

"Here! Here! Oh, please hurry! The fire is awful close and I can't move! Help me! Please!"

Fargo had it now. She was slightly to the north. He gigged the Ovaro, which, for one of the few times ever, balked. He had to tap his spurs to get the stallion to advance. "Keep yelling."

Periwinkle did, her cries growing more and more frantic.

A gust of wind stirred the smoke, and Fargo saw why.

She was on her side on the ground, her legs pinned from the knees down by a fallen pine. The top of the tree was on fire and the flames were traveling down it toward her. Not only that, but not twenty feet off, the woods were nothing but flames and more flames.

"Help me!"

Vaulting down, Fargo slid his hands under the tree. The bark was warm to his touch. He lifted, or tried to, but it resisted his efforts. "You and your little brother," he muttered.

"What?" she said in confusion, her eyes on the fire.

"Nothing, damn it."

"Hurry!" Periwinkle wailed. Her face was streaked with tears and soot and her hair was a mess. Wild fear lit her eyes as she pushed at the tree, trying to help. "Get me out!"

What did she think he was trying to do? Fargo asked himself in annoyance as he planted his boots and bent his knees and back. He tried again, his neck muscles swelling, his veins bulging. The oak rose but only a few inches. "Crawl out from under!" he bellowed.

"I can't." Periwinkle was staring, petrified, at the approaching inferno.

"You're not even trying," Fargo shouted. "Get out from under it or I'll let go."

Sobbing in fright, Periwinkle dug her elbow in and levered her body clear. "I did it!" Gasping from her effort and the smoke, she collapsed onto her back.

Fargo let go of the tree and sprang to her side. "How bad are your legs? Can you ride?"

"I don't know how bad they are," Periwinkle said, clutching at him. "I can't feel them."

They had no time to waste finding out. Scooping her up, Fargo threw her onto the Ovaro and scrambled on behind her. His arms around her waist so she wouldn't fall off, he reined to the south.

"I came looking for you," Periwinkle said over her shoulder. "But I got lost in all the smoke."

"Figured as much," Fargo said. "Now hush." He had riding to do. They had fire behind them and fire to the right and to the left. Unless they reached the end of the valley quickly, they'd have fire in front of them, too.

As usual, Periwinkle didn't listen. "What about my family? And the rest of my kin?"

"Fine the last I saw them."

Up ahead, flames from the west were leaping from treetop to treetop with unnerving swiftness. So far only the high canopy was ablaze, but it wouldn't stay that way. Glowing embers rained down. So did more than a few burning branches.

"Watch out!" Periwinkle cried.

With a rending crash, a large limb over their heads gave way. Fargo reined aside barely in time.

"That was close," Periwinkle gasped.

Fargo skirted a smoldering thicket and reined up short in consternation. They were a still ways from Granville's clearing—and the woods ahead were combusting like kindling in a campfire.

# 43

Even as Fargo looked, several trees burst into flame. He could see what appeared to be gaps, although it was hard to tell with so much smoke, and made for one at a trot.

Periwinkle suddenly screamed and pointed.

A tall pine, half its limbs ablaze, was toppling toward them. Sparks and fireballs flew from it like molten hail.

Hauling on the reins, Fargo raced for safety. There was a resounding thud, and he swore the ground under the Ovaro shook. A ball of fire shot at them, almost catching the Ovaro.

Another gap appeared and he was through in the bat of an eye. He didn't slow until they reached the clearing.

"Oh no," Periwinkle wailed.

The cabin was on fire. The roof had caught and hungry flames were licking at the rear wall.

To the east and west the forest was completely engulfed. Behind them, more flames crackled in pursuit.

The only way open was to the south, but streams of red and orange were flowing to close off that escape as well.

"Hold up a minute," Periwinkle said.

"We can't stop," Fargo replied, and didn't.

"But I don't feel good," Periwinkle said. "I don't feel good at all. I'm afraid I might—" She leaned to the side and retched, some of the vomit splashing on his boot.

Fargo had been feeling queasy himself. The smoke was to blame. It got into his belly as well as his lungs.

"Sorry," Periwinkle said, dabbing at her mouth with her sleeve. "I couldn't help myself."

"Hush up." Fargo couldn't afford to be distracted. The fire had swept around the clearing to the southwest. They must make it out before it encircled them.

"Where are my folks?" Periwinkle asked. "Do you think they're safe? If anything has happened to them, I don't know what I'll do." Tears trickled and she uttered a low sob.

Fargo was intent only on the fire. They were almost to the last strip of untouched woodland. Just as they plunged into the vegetation, a tree to their right went up with a loud whoosh. Periwinkle screamed. What with her and the din of the fire and the smoke, it was a wonder Fargo could think. His head hurt and his lungs felt as if they were filled with sand. Even more troubling, the Ovaro was having great difficulty breathing. If the stallion went down, they were as good as dead.

Fargo threaded through small spruce, went up a low knoll, and stopped.

For some reason the air above the knoll was momentarily clear of smoke. The panorama that unfolded was enough to spike fear through anyone.

To the north the valley was roiling fire. Granville's cabin had been turned into a log bonfire. The mountain to the east was being devoured, slope by ever-higher slope, as the flames climbed toward the crest. West of the valley, the fire was overrunning everything in its path. Smoke filled the sky from horizon to horizon.

"Look at all that!" Periwinkle exclaimed in terror. "Why are we sittin' here? Get us out!"

Fargo trotted down the knoll. Once again, they were smothered in smoke. Eager to be shed of it, he rode faster than was safe.

Periwinkle pressed against his chest to steady herself, sniffling.

Fargo kept hoping to catch a glimpse of the others, but they had too much of a lead. He passed between a pair of ponderosas and had to rein up once again. Before them stretched a phalanx of fir, on fire. The boles were so closely spaced that making it through unscathed was out of the question.

"Go east," Periwinkle urged. "We can avoid it."

Fargo was already on the move. His worry now was that the eastern and western arms of the fire would join before they made it out. Swatting at the smoke, he had his most violent coughing fit yet.

So did Periwinkle. "I can't take much more of this," she wheezed. "I feel sick and light-headed."

"We'll make it," Fargo assured her with more conviction than he felt.

"I don't want to die. Not now. Not when I have so much to live for."

Fargo let her ramble. It took her mind off the danger they were in, and calmed her a little.

"I want to live so you and me can be man and wife. You've shown me what life is all about."

"Not that again," Fargo snapped. He couldn't help himself.

"I don't care how mad you get," Periwinkle said. "I want to give myself to you every night for the rest of our lives."

"Damn it, girl," Fargo said.

"You like me. I know you do. Or you wouldn't have taken me off in the woods like you did and—"

Fargo was spared from having to listen to more of her silliness by another coughing fit. Doubling over the saddle horn, Periwinkle hacked and quaked and tried to suck in air that wasn't there.

"No more talking," he cautioned. "It'll only make things worse."

Periwinkle nodded.

A gust of wind sent flames licking at them from the west. Fargo avoided them, but it put the Ovaro closer to the fire to the east. They were caught in the middle and the middle was shrinking.

A burning tree fell against another and both swayed precariously. A sparrow flew past, from east to west, and as it neared a bush, both the bush and the sparrow burst into flame.

"The heat," Periwinkle gasped. "How can you stand it?"

Fargo barely could. Squinting against the smoke, his teeth gritted, he had to do all he could to stay in the saddle. The Ovaro was on the verge of collapse, too. He decided to take a desperate gamble. Reluctantly bringing the stallion to a gallop, he sought to escape the fire before they were brought down.

Periwinkle let out a wail and went limp against him. She would have fallen if not for his arm around her waist.

The Ovaro sounded liked a blacksmith's bellows. The stallion's own desperation was evident in its wide eyes and flared nostrils.

"Come on, big fella," Fargo said through his bandanna, patting its neck. "We can do this."

Prongs of flame were converging from the west and the east. Fargo couldn't be sure because his vision was so blurred, but it appeared that the wind was driving the flames faster than ever.

Suffering intensely, Fargo sped for their lives.

Unexpectedly, Periwinkle stirred and straightened. "What?" she blurted in confusion. "Where are we?"

Fargo was too focused on riding to answer.

"Oh God. We're not out of it yet?"

"Sit still, damn it," Fargo growled. She was squirming so much he was about to lose his grip.

Periwinkle suddenly pointed and shrieked, "Look! We're cut off!"

Fargo raised his head to see better, thinking that it couldn't be, not yet.

But she was right.

# 44

With all his worry over the fires to the east and west merging, Fargo hadn't considered another threat. Namely, that the wind would blow burning embers and set the woods ahead on fire, too. That was exactly what had happened. And once ignited, the flames had spread in a long line that effectively blocked the only way out.

"What do we do?" Periwinkle wailed.

Fargo drew rein. Fire to the right; fire to the left; fire in front; fire behind. They were trapped and would soon be dead unless he could think of a way to escape. But for once his quick wits failed him. Short of plunging into the fire ahead and hoping for the best, he couldn't think of anything.

They couldn't just sit there, either.

He reined to the west for about twenty yards, seeking a gap, no matter how small. There wasn't any. He reined eastward and went twice as far. Still nothing. He was about to circle around when without warning the ground opened up in front of them, and the Ovaro stumbled and nearly went down.

At first Fargo thought it was a gully and went to rein around. Then he noticed the rock walls. It was a small ravine, barely wide enough for the stallion. On an impulse he rode down in. Almost immediately there was less smoke. The sides rose above them. Six feet. Ten feet. Then they were at the bottom and they could breathe without coughing. He drew rein.

"What are you doing?" Periwinkle asked. "We can't stop. We have to keep goin' and find a way out."

Fargo looked down. There was no brush, not even any grass. Only rock and dirt. And most of the smoke was being blown over them. "It might work," he said.

"What might?" Periwinkle asked in a panic. Twisting, she gripped his arm. "Get us out of here."

"No."

Periwinkle glanced up. "What are you thinkin'? That the fire might not reach us down here?"

That was exactly what Fargo was thinking. "There's nothing down here that can burn."

"Except us."

"It's our only hope."

"You're a fool," Periwinkle said harshly. "It'll kill us as sure as anything. A tree will fall on us or we'll suffocate."

"You'd better hope we don't."

Periwinkle yanked on his arm. "Damn you. Take us out of here before it's too late."

"It already is," Fargo said, and nodded upward.

The fire had reached them. Flames were visible, shooting along the west rim. The roar filled their ears, and the heat was withering. Barely a moment later flames appeared on the east rim. The smoke grew thicker.

Fargo felt the Ovaro quake, and he didn't blame it. He was afraid, too.

Periwinkle was in the grip of abject fright, her mouth opening and closing but no sounds coming out.

Crackling, snapping, and popping rose in a tremendous din. The thud of toppled trees was near continuous.

Burning pieces struck close above and broke into tiny showers.

Crying out, Periwinkle buried her face in Fargo's chest. "I can't stand it!" she screeched. "I just can't stand it!"

Her fear made the Ovaro shift uneasily, and Fargo gave him a few pats. "Easy," he said quietly. "Easy."

A flaming leaf fell and Fargo swatted it aside. Tense with expectation, he waited for something worse to happen. All it would take was for a tree to fall into the ravine. But gradually the roar lessened, the crackling diminished. The heat wasn't as blistering.

Even better, Periwinkle stopped sobbing and raised her tear-and-snot-streaked face. "Can it be?" she said, and wiped her nose with her sleeve. "Did we do it?"

"We?" Fargo said.

"Listen! It sounds like the fire is movin' away." Beaming, she smacked the saddle horn in delight. "We should go find the others."

"Not yet."

Periwinkle placed her hands on her hips. "Why in blazes not? The worst is over, isn't it?"

"Use your damn head. It's still too hot up there. We have to wait until things cool down."

"When will that be? And why are you cussin' at me?"

"Because you have the brains of a tree stump," Fargo said bluntly. "We'll go when I say and not before."

That shut her up for a while.

Fargo wouldn't mind climbing down and resting, but there wasn't room to dismount. The ravine walls were brushing against his legs.

Periwinkle sulked. She was a great little sulker. Her lips pursed as if she'd sucked on a lemon, she'd glare at him awhile, look away, and glare at him some more. The next time she did it, he puckered his own lips and blew her a kiss.

"I don't think I like you so much anymore," she declared.

"Lucky me."

"Why are you bein' so mean? Is it because of how I acted? I was scared. Practically beside myself."

"You didn't stay with the others like I told you to do. You went and got lost in the smoke and I had to come look for you."

"That's all you're mad about?"

"You nearly got us burned alive."

"But we weren't. We survived. And now things can go on as they were." Periwinkle hugged him, pressing her cheek to his chest. "You and me. Man and wife. I can't wait."

Fargo decided he might as well get it over with. "Not ever," he said.

Drawing back, Periwinkle said, "You've changed your mind about marryin' me? Over a little thing like this?"

"It's not so little. And I never said I would in the first place. But that's not the real reason."

"Then what is?" Periwinkle demanded. "After I went and gave myself to you?"

"Quit throwing that in my face. You're not the first woman to make love."

"What possible excuse can you have for not wantin' to marry me?"

"You're a bitch."

Astonishment rendered her speechless. Then, sputtering, almost purple with fury, she poked him in the chest. "How dare you! I have the sweetest disposition any woman ever had. Just ask my ma. She tells me that all the time."

"She lies to spare your feelings."

Periwinkle balled her fists. "You . . . you . . ." She couldn't seem to find the right word. "I hate you now. Do you hear me? I wouldn't marry you if you were the last man left on earth. What do you say to that?"

Fargo looked at the sky. "I'm obliged," he said.

# 45

Over an hour went by before Fargo deemed it safe enough to gig the Ovaro to the top of the ravine. He was careful not to leave the shelter of the rock walls until he had looked around.

The forest was no more. Every tree, every bush, every blade of grass had been reduced to a blackened ruin. Charred stumps stood like gravestones, hundreds and hundreds stretching in all directions. Ash was everywhere. Smoke still rose from the stumps, from the crisped brush, from the ground itself.

"Can we go now?" Periwinkle asked impatiently.

"When I say so." Fargo rode out and stopped again. Sliding down, he placed a hand on the ground.

"What are you doin'?"

"Seeing how hot it is."

"What does it matter? We're safe up on your horse."

"It's him I'm thinking of." Fargo moved his hand around. The ground was warm. It should be safe enough.

"I'm glad I learned how you are before I made the worst mistake of my life," Periwinkle said scornfully. "What sort of man cares for his horse more than he does for the woman who loves him?"

Fargo didn't dignify the question with an answer. Rising, he climbed back on and proceeded with caution.

"I mean, a horse is just a horse. But a human bein' is special. My pa would never care for his horse more than he does for my ma."

"One day you'll find a man who cares for you more," Fargo said to mollify her. He pitied the poor fool who did.

"It can still be you. I can forgive and forget as good as the next woman. Say you're sorry, and we can start over."

"Get this through your head," Fargo said. "When I'm done here, I'm lighting a shuck." And if he never set eyes on her again, that would be perfectly all right by him.

Crestfallen, Periwinkle bowed her head. "You've crushed my heart, you brute. I don't know how I'll ever recover."

"Shouldn't you be worried about something else right about now?"

"What, for instance?"

"Your family and your kin."

A startled look came over her. "Oh," she exclaimed, and twisted from side to side. "Where can they be? What if they were caught in the fire, too? They could all be dead, and here I am, thinkin' only of myself."

"There's hope for you yet," Fargo said.

It was slow going. They had to avoid burning stumps and clumps of brush and hot spots in the ground itself. They could breathe again, but with every breath the acrid smell of the aftermath saturated their lungs.

At one point Periwinkle sniffed her sleeve and remarked, "I don't reckon I'll ever get this smell out of my clothes."

The fire had traveled to the southeast, the direction they had to go. Fargo imagined it would keep on until it reached Flathead Lake. They were halfway there when he discovered that a change in the wind had caused the flames to sweep to the south.

A swath of woodland half a mile wide had been reduced to cinders.

Fargo kept on to the southeast. It felt strange being in normal woods again.

"We never had fires like this back to Tennessee," Periwinkle remarked. "I've never seen or heard of the like. How common are they?"

Fargo shrugged. "How would I know?" Fires in remote regions were hardly ever written about in the newspapers, even ones as big as this.

"I see your point," Periwinkle said. "If we weren't here, no whites would ever know this happened unless the Injuns told them."

Fargo rose in the stirrups, hoping to spot the rest.

"From now on, summers here will worry me, it's so blamed dry," Periwinkle said. "I wonder if Oregon country is the same. I hear tell they get more rain out thataway."

"In the winter months. The summers are as bad as here."

"Well, tarnation," Periwinkle said. "How's my family goin' to find a safe place to live?"

"If you want safe," Fargo said, "you should have stayed east of the Mississippi River."

"Oh, pshaw. Everybody warned us it was dangerous to come, but except for those no-account outlaws and now this fire we haven't had a lick of trouble."

The woods were unnaturally still. Fargo did see a finch high in a tree and a young rabbit bounded out of hiding to stare at them, something an older rabbit would never do.

"Oh, look!" Periwinkle had seen it, too. "Shoot it so we can have it for supper. There's nothin' I like more than rabbit stew."

"No."

"Why not? Don't tell me the big, brave scout has a soft spot for bunnies and such," Periwinkle taunted.

"Sound can carry a long way."

"And you're worried the outlaws might hear or maybe some hostiles?" Periwinkle snorted in derision. "They don't scare me none."

"Not like fires do," Fargo said.

"You can go to hell. At least with outlaws and hostiles, you can fight back. There's not much you can do in a fire."

"That's as good an excuse as any."

Periwinkle's jaw muscles twitched. "No doubt about it. I have decided I plumb hate you."

A rise blocked their view of the stretch of forest before the lake. Rather than climb it and tire the Ovaro even more, Fargo went around. He stayed close to where the slope met the woods, where the going was easier.

"Why haven't we caught up by now?" Periwinkle complained. "We must be gettin' close."

"You are, missy," a man declared, and from behind a wide pine stepped Kline and another outlaw.

# 46

Fargo's natural instinct was to grab for his Colt, but both their rifles were pointed at his chest. He drew rein, holding his hands where they could see them.

"It's the outlaws!" Periwinkle exclaimed, and went to jump off the Ovaro.

Kline swung his rifle on her. "What do you think you're doin', you nitwit? Try to run and we'll gun you."

"You'd shoot a female?" Periwinkle said.

"In a heartbeat, you stupid cow." Kline sidled around to the side of the Ovaro. "Bet you didn't count on seein' us again so soon, did you, scout?"

"I was hoping the fire got you," Fargo admitted.

"We lit out before it came anywhere close," Kline said. "Saw the homesteaders runnin' for their lives and followed 'em. They're over that rise, yonder, about a quarter mile or so."

"Where's Latham?"

"He had a powerful hankerin' for that yellow-haired filly. It made him mad as anything when you took her from us."

"Are you talkin' about my cousin Darlene?" Periwinkle asked.

"You know of any other blond fillies hereabouts?" Kline replied. "Latham has always been partial to yellow hair. He can't stand the sight of black hair."

"*I* have black hair," Periwinkle said.

"Which is why he'd never give you a poke." Kline put a hand on her leg. "Me, on the other hand. I don't give a damn what color a gal's hair is. All I care about is spreadin' her legs and goin' at it."

"You're despicable."

"Now, now. Treat me nice and I might let you live," Kline said, and cackled. "But it would have to be *real* nice, if you get my drift."

Fargo knew better. They weren't about to allow either of them to go on breathing. Somehow he must pull on them before they shot him from the saddle. "If her kin are that close, they'll hear the shots."

"Let them," Kline said. "By the time they get here, Rosten and me will be long gone. Ain't that right, Rosten?"

The other outlaw nodded.

"I can kill you and poke her and make my day complete," Kline said. "Any last words before I get to it?"

"You try stickin' your dingus in me and I'll cut it off," Periwinkle vowed.

Kline laughed. "I'm shakin' in my boots. You're the fearsomest female I've ever seen."

The outlaw called Rosten thought that was hilarious.

"Climb down, girl, so we can get to it," Kline said.

"I will not," Periwinkle replied.

"Damn, you're dumb. It's like this, girl. I aim to shoot that son of a bitch behind you. Now, you can get off his cayuse and I shoot him out of that saddle, or you can be stubborn and sit up there and I'll shoot through you to hit him."

Periwinkle looked over her shoulder at Fargo. Sadness came into her eyes and she said, "I'm sorry."

"Do what you have to," Fargo said.

"I intend to." Gripping the saddle horn, Periwinkle slid to the ground. She smoothed her dress, fluffed with her hair, and stepped in front of Kline. "Here I am, just like you wanted."

"You're between me and his horse," Kline said, wagging his six-shooter. "Move out of the way so I can shoot him."

Instead Periwinkle moved closer to Kline, an odd smile on her face. "Don't you want a kiss first?"

"What?"

"A kiss and maybe a whole lot more," Periwinkle said, and tossed her hips suggestively.

Kline had momentarily forgotten about Fargo. "What are you playin' at, girl?" he asked suspiciously.

"You want a poke. I want a poke. Everybody wants a poke," Periwinkle said.

"The bitch is loco," Rosten said.

"I'm no such thing," Periwinkle replied. "Ask the scout. He'll tell you how much I wanted a poke. Go ahead. Ask him."

Kline tore his gaze from her. "What's she talkin' about?"

"It's true," Fargo said. "She's been begging me for one for more than a day now. I keep saying no, but she keeps at it."

"You told her no?" Kline said in amazement.

"He doesn't want to poke me," Periwinkle said. "I about got down on my knees, and he still wouldn't."

"What kind of man says no to that?" Kline said.

"Both of them are loco," Rosten threw in. He had lowered his rifle a few inches, but the barrel was still pointed in Fargo's direction.

"What do you say?" Periwinkle said to Kline. "Do I have to beg you for a poke, too?"

"Hell, girl," Kline said. "I was fixin' to rape you, and now you say you'll let me do it with no fuss?"

"As many times as you want," Periwinkle said.

"This is a trick."

"We have a sayin' back in Tennessee," Periwinkle said. "Never look a gift horse in the mouth. Well, you're lookin'. I had my first poke the other day, and I like it. I like it a lot. I want more. What's so hard to understand about that? Don't you like pokes, too?"

"Sure I do, damn it," Kline said, sounding confused. "But women aren't supposed to come right out and say they want you to poke them."

"Oh, posh," Periwinkle said. "Fallen doves do it all the time."

"But you're no whore. You're just a girl."

"Aren't I pretty?"

"Pretty as hell," Kline said.

"Don't you want me?"

"Why is it females ask such stupid damn questions? You make me hard just lookin' at you."

"Yet there you stand and here I stand and your hands aren't anywhere on me. When it comes to pokes, you're downright pitiful. Almost as pitiful as him." Periwinkle turned and gestured at Fargo and winked.

Neither Kline nor Rosten saw her do it.

"Don't this beat all?" Kline said. "I wish more females were as accommodatin' as you are."

"Are we goin' to shoot the scout or not?" Rosten asked.

Kline was staring at Periwinkle's breasts and licking his lips. "Shoot him anytime you want. I have me some pokin' to do." And leering, he reached for her.

# 47

Fargo had to hand it to Periwinkle Calloway. She had used her feminine wiles on Kline as slickly as any lady of the night in Denver or New Orleans. Kline was so befuddled he lowered his rifle to his side.

Rosten, though, started to raise his again.

Fargo drew his Colt and fanned two shots. The slugs slammed Rosten back. With a cry of rage he tried to take aim and Fargo shot him a third time, square in the center of the forehead. Hair and brains sprayed, and the outlaw collapsed.

Fargo was in motion even as he fired the third shot. He dived from the Ovaro, cocking the Colt as he went, wanting a clear shot at Kline. He didn't get it.

Lunging, Kline grabbed Periwinkle, spun her around, and clamped an arm around her throat. With her as a shield, he backed toward the woods, leveling his rifle at Fargo.

Kline fired as Fargo hit the ground on his shoulder. The shot missed. Another moment, and Kline had pulled Periwinkle into the trees.

Fargo heaved up after them. He went a dozen feet and crouched but didn't see them.

A thicket a few yards away rustled and Fargo caught a glimpse of Periwinkle, her hand beckoning in appeal. He ran after them but had to spring for cover when the muzzle of Kline's rifle was thrust at him. He flattened as the rifle spat lead and smoke.

Kline's mount must be back in there somewhere, and Fargo had to stop him from reaching it. He charged in pursuit.

The rifle boomed, but Kline missed, and Fargo heard thrashing and other sounds of a struggle.

Kline cursed a mean streak.

Bursting through some brush, Fargo nearly tripped over them.

Periwinkle and Kline were locked in a struggle. She had hold of the rifle and was desperately trying to wrest it from Kline's grasp while Kline twisted and wrenched and couldn't stop swearing.

Fargo aimed the Colt at Kline's head, but they rolled toward him. He went to bound aside and they slammed into his shins. The next moment he was on his hands and knees. In the selfsame instant Kline tore his rifle free and drove the stock at Fargo's head. Fargo jerked away, but his temple exploded in pain and the world spun around him.

"No!" Periwinkle cried.

The sounds of their struggle were renewed.

Fargo rose onto his knees in time to see Kline club her. Without missing a beat, Kline sprang, swinging the rifle at Fargo's face. Fargo got his arms up to block the blow, and excruciating pain speared from his wrists to his elbows. He tried to point the Colt, but his arm wouldn't move as it should.

Kline was scrambling back, levering a round into the chamber. Fargo went after him and swatted the barrel aside as the rifle went off. Then he had hold of Kline's wrist and Kline had hold of his.

"You son of a bitch!" Kline snarled.

They fought in savage fury. Kline rammed a knee at Fargo's groin, but Fargo shifted and took it on his thigh. He returned the favor, and Kline grunted and sputtered and turned red.

Without warning they rolled against a tree. Fargo's back was to the trunk, and he lost his hat. Kline, hissing like a snake, tried to bite him in the throat. Fargo retaliated by butting his forehead into Kline's mouth, pulping Kline's lips and causing blood to pour.

Kline growled like a wild beast.

Fargo butted him again and teeth crunched. He butted Kline a third time, in the nose.

Yowling in pain, Kline suddenly let go, tore loose of Fargo's grasp, and clawed for his six-shooter. He nearly had it out when Fargo shoved the Colt into his ribs and squeezed the trigger. Kline recoiled, clutched at Fargo's Colt, and Fargo shot him again.

Kline's hands went limp and his six-gun plopped in the grass.

Red rivulets trickling from his nose, he had to try twice to spit out "Bastard."

Rising, Fargo kicked Kline's revolver out of reach. A groan from Periwinkle drew him to her side. She was unconscious, a swelling goose egg on her temple. He slid his arm under her to sit her up.

A feeling seized him, a sense of danger. The instinct was so strong he glanced over his shoulder.

Kline had somehow made it to his knees and was slinking toward him with a dagger in his hand. Where the dagger came from, Fargo couldn't say, unless it had been under Kline's shirt.

The instant Fargo looked, Kline sprang. Kline's wounds slowed him, but he still nearly sliced Fargo's neck open as, letting go of Periwinkle, Fargo threw himself aside.

Kline came after him, stabbing in a frenzy.

Scrambling back, Fargo saved himself. Kline came on, his features set in grim concentration; he was determined to kill Fargo before he succumbed to his wounds.

Fargo kicked at Kline's knife hand, but Kline jerked it away.

"No, you don't," Kline spat, blood spraying from his mouth.

Fargo pointed the Colt, but Kline swatted it with the dagger. Drawing back his leg, Fargo kicked him in the chest.

Kline was knocked flat but came up again, swaying. He raised the dagger. "Kill you!" he exclaimed.

Fargo shot him in the chest.

Pitching to his knees, Kline dropped his weapon. His chin drooped. He took a deep breath and got out a blubbery "Bastard."

Fargo set to reloading.

"You've done killed me."

"Doesn't sound like you're dead to me." Fargo picked up the dagger.

Kline managed to raise his head. "Do it, you son of a bitch. Don't let me suffer like this."

About to thrust the dagger into Kline's heart, Fargo shook his head and tossed it to the ground. "No," he said. Moving to Periwinkle, he finished replacing the spent cartridges.

Kline's eyes were pools of hate. "You'd do this to a white man?"

"What does that have to do with it?" Fargo said. "Pricks come in all colors."

Wheezing noisily, Kline did a strange thing; he smiled. "That's all right. I can die knowin' that if I couldn't beat you, Latham has."

"Beat me how?"

"You'll find out. He's smarter than me. Smarter than most everybody."

"He's a regular genius," Fargo said. "That's why he robs and kills for a living."

"He'll show you," Kline said weakly. "He'll show all of them." Slowly folding at the waist, he came to rest with his forehead on the ground and his arms limp in front of him. "Finish me, damn you."

"You don't deserve the mercy."

Behind Fargo, Periwinkle said, "I'll show him some." She stepped past Fargo, one hand pressed to the goose egg on her temple, the other holding Kline's dagger. Before Fargo could guess her intent, she seized Kline by his hair and yanked his head up.

Kline's eyelids were fluttering. He was almost gone.

"Here's your mercy, you polecat," Periwinkle said, and buried the dagger in his throat.

Kline stiffened and collapsed.

Smiling, Periwinkle stepped back. "That's what a man deserves for wantin' to poke a woman without her say-so. Don't you agree?"

"Either that or cut his pecker off."

Periwinkle blinked. "Dang. Why didn't I think of that?"

"Do you think you really could?" Fargo asked skeptically.

"I don't rightly know," Periwinkle replied, "but it would be fun to find out." And she laughed merrily.

# 48

Kline hadn't lied. The Tennesseans were camped less than a quarter of a mile beyond the rise. Food was being cooked. Some of the older boys were serving as lookouts, and when one spied the Ovaro and hollered, the men came on the run.

Lester was foremost, hobbling like a madman. Spreading his arms wide, he embraced Periwinkle, tears of joys moistening his cheeks. "Daughter, daughter," he said. "You had your ma and me worried sick."

Priscilla hurried up and hugged both of them. "Praise the Lord," she said, adding her tears to her husband's.

Leading the Ovaro by the reins, Fargo walked to the fire. He figured the rest would be as elated, but Granville and Rufus and the other adults were as somber as death.

"It's Darlene," Granville said when Fargo asked what was wrong. He had an arm over Charlotte's shoulders, and it was obvious Charlotte had been crying. "She's been taken."

"Latham," Fargo said, remembering Kline's boast.

Granville nodded, and Charlotte groaned.

"It was the most brazen thing you ever saw," Rufus said, "him snatchin' her in front of our eyes."

"You *saw* him do it?" Fargo said.

"How could we not?" Rufus rejoined. "We'd just made camp and were sittin' around the fire, waitin' for you and Lester's girl to show. We figured to give you an hour and if you didn't, go lookin'."

Vernon took up the account. "Our women had just got done bandagin' everyone who got burned, and we were all so wore out we weren't payin' much attention to what was goin' on around us."

"That's when that damn outlaw waltzed up as bold as you please and shoved his pistol in Darlene's face," Rufus said.

"No one saw him until it was too late," Solomon mentioned.

"He came around the horses," Rufus said. "Sneakylike."

Granville had to cough before he could relate what happened next. "He told us he was takin' her. Said if we followed, he'd splatter her brains. His very words."

"It's his'n that need to be splattered," Rufus said.

"That wasn't all." Granville looked Fargo in the eye. "He said to tell you that she was bait. That he didn't give a damn about her. The one he wants is you."

"He aims to kill you," Rufus said.

"He's expectin' you to go after him," Granville said. "Told us if you didn't, he'll kill her. He said you're to go alone. Said if you didn't, he'll kill her. He said that he'll be waitin' somewhere along the lake, and if you take too long—"

"He'll kill her," Fargo finished for him.

Charlotte wrung her hands and sniffled. "I begged him not to. I asked him to take me and not my daughter, and do you know what he did?"

"He laughed."

"You'd have thought it was a great joke. He said why should he take the old mare when he can have the young filly?"

"If I could've gotten my hands on him . . . ," Granville said, and bunched his fists so tight his knuckles popped.

"That varmint has a powerful hate for you, mister," Rufus said. "He blames you for destroyin' his gang, as he put it. Says he won't leave this neck of the country until you're food for the worms."

"I reckon I'd better head out, then," Fargo said.

Vernon drew a sharp glare from Charlotte by saying, "You look plumb tuckered. Why not rest for five or ten minutes? There's coffee ready if you'd like some."

"He should go now," Charlotte said.

"A few more won't make a difference," Vernon insisted.

Fargo nipped their argument in the bud with "A cup of coffee won't make much of a difference, either." Turning, he forked leather. "If I'm not back by midnight, odds are I'll never be. Wait until first light and head out after him yourselves. It could be he won't harm her so long as he can use her to keep you at bay." That last was for Charlotte's benefit. He doubted Latham would let Darlene live once Latham did him in.

"Go with God," Charlotte said.

"Hold on," Granville said. "Why let that owl hoot hold all the cards? Leave marks for us to see and we'll follow after you and maybe lend a hand when you catch up to him."

"Like the dickens you will," Charlotte said. "It's apt to get Darlene killed. That outlaw is bound to be watchin' his back trail."

"She's right," Fargo said. "It has to be me and only me."

"I hate this," Granville said. "That girl is my own flesh and blood and I can't lift a finger to save her."

"Be looking for us," Fargo said, and headed out.

The lake was about an hour away. As much as Fargo would like to ride like the wind, he held the Ovaro to a walk. The stallion was exhausted from all they'd been through. Push too hard and it might give out on him.

He wasn't surprised that Latham hadn't fanned the breeze for parts unknown.

The man must want to kill him in the worst way. But that was all right. He wanted to put an end to Latham, too.

It was a while before the lake appeared, shimmering in the heat.

Fargo rode to the top of a last low hill close to the water and scoured the shore for sign of Latham and Darlene. He saw something else. Smoke from several campfires, rising to the south. It must be Captain Benson and the patrol. With all that had happened, Fargo had completely forgotten about them. Benson must think he was dead. And he couldn't spare the time to go explain the situation.

Not with Darlene in that killer's clutches.

The patrol's presence helped in one respect. Now he knew that Latham hadn't gone south and risked running into them.

Riding to the water's edge, Fargo turned north. No sooner did he do so than he came across the tracks of a pair of shod horses.

Fargo gigged the Ovaro.

Latham had stuck close to the lake where the trail would be plain. Making it easy for him, Fargo reflected, to ride into Latham's gun sight.

That much he expected.

What he didn't expect was the sight that awaited him when he came around a headland and saw a bluff that overlooked the lake. A lone tree stood near the brink. And under it, with a noose around her neck, was Darlene.

# 49

Fargo's first thought was that Latham had hanged her. He used his spurs and wound up a game trail to the summit. The tree blocked his view. Dreading the worst, he reined around it.

Darlene's ankles were bound and her wrists tied behind her back. She had been gagged, and was perched on a small boulder, the rope around her neck so taut she was forced to stand on the tips of her toes to keep from being strangled. She had heard him, and twisted her face around. Tears filled her eyes and she nearly lost her balance.

"Hold on," Fargo said, swinging from the saddle. "I'll have you free in a minute."

"Try and I shoot her," said a voice as cold as ice.

Fargo froze.

Latham had risen from behind a larger boulder a dozen steps off, his six-shooter out and cocked. "Now, don't you twitch, you hear?"

Fargo was surprised Latham hadn't shot him on sight. But then again, some outlaws liked to play with those they were about to snuff out, like a cat playing with a mouse.

"Nothin' to say?" Latham taunted.

"She has no part in this. Let her go."

"Aren't you sweet? But you know better. I aim to have some fun with her as soon as Kline and Rosten get here. Course, you'll be dead by then. Maybe I'll do her next to your dead body."

Fargo almost gave a start. Latham didn't know about his pards. A desperate brainstorm sparked him to say, "How about a trade instead?"

"You have nothin' I want."

"The cavalry does."

"What do they have to do with this?"

"You know the patrol is camped back on the lake shore, don't you?"

"I spotted them not long after I took the girl. It's why I came this way instead of swingin' south as I'd planned. So what?"

"So they have your friends."

"You're lyin'. Kline wouldn't be dumb enough to go anywhere near them."

"He didn't," Fargo said. "I got the jump on the two of them and turned them over to the captain in charge before I came after you."

Latham came around the boulder, his face coloring with anger. "I should shoot you where you stand."

"You do, and Kline and Rosten will end up in prison, or hanged."

"God, I hate you," Latham said.

"How about that trade? Them for Darlene."

"You got the jump on them, you claim?" Latham said. It was plain he wasn't convinced.

"They were watching the homesteaders." Fargo embellished his lie. "I got lucky and spotted them before they saw me. They didn't hear me sneak up on them. I had to shoot Rosten in the leg and they dropped their hardware. The rest was easy."

Latham's jaw muscles twitched.

"What do you say?" Fargo pressed him.

"You miserable, rotten son of a bitch."

"Do I take that as yes?"

"Damn Kline, anyhow."

"Her life for theirs. I call that a good swap."

"Shut the hell up. I need to think." Latham's brow puckered. He glanced at Darlene, then at the faintly visible smoke from the army camp. "Kline never could do anything right. I've always had to hold his damn hand."

Darlene was teetering and might slip off the boulder at any moment.

"You don't have all day to make up your mind," Fargo said quickly. "If she dies, they can hang for all I care."

"I told you to shut up," Latham snapped. His face twisted in indecision, he finally swore and said, "Get her down. We'll do the trade. But any tricks and both of you are dead."

"I'll need a knife," Fargo said. He didn't want Latham to know about the Arkansas toothpick.

"Just climb on your horse and untie her," Latham said. "Shuck your gun belt first."

Fargo pried at the buckle and let it drop. Turning, he swung onto the Ovaro and reined over next to Darlene. Steadying her with his shoulder, he worked at undoing the noose.

Latham came nearer, oozing fury. "I had this all worked out. I was goin' to pay you back for all the trouble you've caused me, then head for Oregon country and prey on the settlers up there. Now that fool Kline has spoiled it. I have half a mind to let them have him."

Fargo didn't say anything. He kept trying to loosen the noose and prayed Latham would venture closer still.

"The settlers in Oregon country have to be better off than this bunch. They hardly had anything worth stealin'. But how was I to know they were so dirt-poor?"

Fargo had the impression Latham was talking to himself, not to them. "Hang on," he whispered to Darlene, then winced at his poor choice of words.

"Maybe I should do the swap," Latham babbled on, "just so I can pistol-whip Kline for bein' a jackass and gettin' himself caught."

"Can I take the gag out of her mouth?" Fargo asked.

"Leave it in." Latham gestured impatiently. "What's takin' so long? It's a slipknot, for God's sake."

"You tied it too tight," Fargo said. "I can't get it to move."

"I do tie good knots," Latham said.

Careful not to knock Darlene off the boulder, Fargo tugged harder. She looked at him with mute appeal in her eyes.

"I should have given you the knife out of my saddlebags," Latham said. "Hurry it the hell up."

"I'm trying," Fargo said. He truly was. He needed the noose off Darlene before he could make his move.

"I'll have to recruit some new men once I get to Oregon. Better ones than the last. They weren't much as pistol shots and only fair hands with a rifle. Good killers are hard to find these days."

The noose finally came loose, but instead of sliding it over Darlene's head, Fargo put his lips to her ear. "I'm going to jump him. Be ready."

Darlene's eyes widened, and she gave a slight nod.

"I never should have come up this way," Latham was grousing. "I heard about the homesteaders at Fort Laramie and figured they'd be easy pickin's. I didn't count on you comin' along."

"I almost have it," Fargo said, pretending to tug. At the same time, he slid his boots free of his stirrups.

"You're bein' too damn gentle. Tear it off, and if you take some skin, who the hell cares?"

"I'm trying not to hurt her."

Latham snorted. "You must be one of those who thinks females are delicate flowers. They're not. They're dumb bitches."

"There are dumb sons of bitches, too."

"And you're one of them. I have half a mind to . . ." Latham stopped and stared at the lake. "What in hell is that?"

Directly out from the bluff, a huge shadow had appeared just under the surface. The shape was unmistakable. It was a fish of some kind, swimming slowly.

"I should feed you two to that thing," Latham said, and laughed.

Fargo's moment had come. "Now," he whispered to Darlene, and throwing the noose off, he whipped his feet up onto his saddle, poised for a heartbeat, and launched himself at Latham.

The outlaw started to whirl just as Fargo slammed into him. They went down hard and Latham's six-gun went skittering. Enraged, Latham pushed erect and aimed a vicious kick at Fargo's face as he was rising. Fargo blocked it and drove his fist at Latham's gut, but Latham sidestepped and came in swinging. A punch caught Fargo on the neck. He nearly blacked out. Backpedaling, Fargo got his fists up to protect himself, only to see Latham glance at his discarded gun belt and dart toward it.

Fargo took two strides and dived, tackling Latham to keep him from reaching it. Latham swore and boxed at Fargo's head. Fargo landed a blow to the ribs that didn't have any effect.

Latham scrambled onto a knee and Fargo lunged, grabbing him by the ankle. Wrenching free, Latham threw himself at the gun belt. It was just out of his reach.

Fargo hurled himself on top, thinking to pin him. But Latham was as slippery as a snake. He wriggled and pushed and was free again, and now his outstretched fingers weren't an inch from Fargo's Colt. Levering up, Fargo clamped a hand onto Latham's chin. Fargo went to slug him, but an elbow to the groin doubled him over. The pain was excruciating.

Fargo tried to rise, but couldn't. He heard a click and looked up into the muzzle of his own Colt, with Latham's smirking face above it.

"I've changed my mind about that trade. I want to kill you too damn much to let anything stop me."

There was movement behind Latham, and then a thud.

Darlene was still tied at the wrists and ankles, but she had gotten her arms around in front of her and hopped over and beaned Latham with a rock.

Swearing luridly, Latham cuffed her.

By then Fargo had his hand in his boot. With all the force in his body, he stabbed the toothpick up and in, and heard Latham grunt.

The outlaw folded like an empty sack of potatoes on top of him, all life gone.

Pushing the body away, Fargo turned.

Darlene was curled on her side, grinning. "Nicely done."

"I'm obliged for the help. He almost had me," Fargo said. "Give me a minute to cut you free and we can head back."

Darlene's grin grew. "What's your hurry?"

**LOOKING FORWARD!**
The following is the opening
section of the next novel in the exciting
Trailsman series from Signet:

**TRAILSMAN #395**
*BLACK HILLS DEATHBLOW*

*Black Hills, Dakota Territory, 1860—where Fargo faces ene-mies on all sides and the greatest threat of all may be his allies.*

*If the situation wasn't so desperate, Skye, I wouldn't have dis-patched a courier to track you down. And if you have one ounce of good sense, you'll tell me to go to blazes. This isn't just another routine contract job: It's a forlorn hope.*

Colonel Stanley Durant's ominous note had plagued Fargo like a toothache since riding out of Chamberlain and following the Missouri River northwest toward Fort Pierre. But one ounce of good sense hadn't nearly the buying power of one ounce of gold, and right now Fargo was light in both pockets.

It was late afternoon by the time he rode into Fort Pierre, the clear fall air starting to bite and the light of late afternoon taking on that mellow richness just before sunset.

*It's a forlorn hope.* The description didn't help Fargo's mood. He felt weary from his hair to his heels, his ass saddle-sore, his belly pinched from hunger. And his mouth was so dry his tongue felt like a dead leaf stuck to the roof of it.

Fort Pierre, he was sorry to note, hadn't changed much since last time he'd ridden through. A fur-trading post on the Missouri, about a hundred and fifty miles east of the Black Hills, it had been purchased a few years back by the U.S. Army. The army had built a dismal garrison above the river, a bonanza for soiled doves, and left the crude frontier trading center intact.

The current trading post was a low, sprawling, one-story structure of cottonwood logs chinked with mud and loopholed for rifles. Fox skins were drying on stretchers outside the door. The westernmost third of the building was a thriving grog-and-flesh shop, and it was here that the Trailsman reined in the Ovaro, swung slowly down, and stretched out the trail kinks before he looped the reins around a bark-covered snorting post.

The tall, broad-shouldered, slim-hipped frontiersman was clad in fringed buckskins, some of the fringes dark with old blood. His weather-bronzed face and short-cropped beard were half in shadow under the brim of a dusty white hat with a bullet hole in the crown. He wore a walnut-gripped, single-action Colt revolver holstered to his shell belt and a long, very consequential Arkansas toothpick in a boot sheath.

When he removed his hat to slap the dust from it, the westering sun ignited alert eyes the deep, bottomless blue of a high-mountain lake.

A water casket squatted at one corner of the building. Fargo lifted the top off and let it dangle by its rope tether while he dipped out a few double handfuls to splash his face. He didn't trust it enough to drink it.

"Maybe some oats tomorrow, old campaigner," he remarked to his pinto stallion as he loosened the cinch and pulled a brass-framed Henry repeating rifle from its saddle scabbard. He looked around for perhaps fifteen seconds before heading into the grog shop.

Fargo paused inside the doorway, letting his eyes adjust to the dark, smoke-choked, foul-smelling interior. It was the only sit-down watering hole between Chamberlain and the Belle Fourche River and crowded with the usual run of hidebound roustabouts and ruffians.

So far nobody had noticed him standing quietly near the door, the Henry dangling muzzle-down from his left hand. But he knew that would likely change before long. Unfortunately for the Trailsman, he had a dangerous and unwanted affliction known as a "reputation," and it wouldn't be long before some drunk-as-a-skunk yahoo decided to measure his dick against that reputation.

### *Excerpt from* **BLACK HILLS DEATHBLOW**

When he could make out the room better, Fargo made his way toward the long plank bar.

"Hey-up, Smedley!" he greeted the barkeep.

"Skye Fargo! It's been a coon's age," replied a man so heavy that his face creased under its own weight. "What's yours?"

"Whiskey with a beer posse."

"The beer's got plenty of bubbles left, but it's warm—the ice-house is empty until the first winter harvest comes in."

"Warm beer's all right. That'll draw nappy."

From the corner of his right eye, Fargo saw that a burly, belligerent-looking drunk wrapped in moth-eaten pelts was watching him with unblinking, trouble-seeking eyes.

Fargo chose to ignore him, casting his gaze around the fly-blown doggery. It was a typical frontier establishment: shoddy-board walls nailed to the logs to help hold the stove heat in, and an uneven floor with several tin spittoons, all but one tipped over. The bullet-holed roof was made of flattened-out cans that had once served for shipping oysters.

The place had the stale, rancid stench of unwashed bodies and cheap popskull. Yet, in Fargo's experience, it was as permanent and elegant as anything else the sprawling and dangerous Dakota Territory had to offer.

Smedley plunked down a shot glass and a chipped beer mug sporting a billowy head. The pelt-clad drunk standing to Fargo's right poked his elbow into a companion's ribs and said something Fargo didn't hear above the raucous din. Both men snickered.

"On the house, damn you," Smedley said when he saw Fargo counting out the last of his five-cent shinplasters. "You go through that routine every time you're broke. You know nobody wants that damn paper money, and that's why you carry it."

Fargo, guilty as charged, couldn't suppress a grin. "'Preciate it, old son."

Fargo picked up the shot glass between thumb and forefinger and peered into it. It was said that safe liquor always reflected a man's eye back. This stuff was like staring into river-bottom mud.

"There's no such thing as ugly women or bad whiskey." Fargo rallied himself before he tossed back the shot and shuddered violently.

"Son of a *bitch*," he told Smedley. "Ain't you got white man's whiskey?"

### *Excerpt from* **BLACK HILLS DEATHBLOW**

"That corpse reviver will make a man outta you, Skye. Whatever don't kill you can only make you stronger, ah?"

Fargo quickly chased the potent concoction with half of the beer. The burly hard case to his right moved in a little closer to Fargo. Fargo didn't spot a firearm in all that tattered fur, but a fifteen-inch, nickel-plated bowie knife protruded from his red sash like an angry serpent.

"My pard here tells me you're Skye Fargo, the jasper some call the Trailsman," he remarked in a hoarse voice laced with scorn. "Might that be the truth?"

"It just might be," Fargo replied amiably. He was starting to feel that pleasant floating sensation as the strong liquor kicked in fast on an empty belly.

"Well, I'm a Dutchman! I ain't never met no storybook hero. They say you've cut a wide swath, yes, they do!"

The drunk had raised his voice to attract an audience. Fargo sipped his beer and said nothing. There was no shortage of assholes on the frontier. . . .

"Yessir!" Fur Boy charged on. "You're a *mighty*-talked-about hombre. But a feller has to wunner 'bout a . . . man with such pretty teeth. 'Specially one that needs to put barley bubbles behind his liquor. Mayhap he belongs back in Vermont running one a them whatchacallits, one a them dancing schools for young ladies."

"Now, let's you and me clarify this matter," Fargo suggested. "You're drunk, so think careful now: Was that remark an insult or just some cracker-barrel wit?"

"You can't figure it out, Buckskins?"

"I just did," Fargo replied as he set his heels hard and side-hammered the man viciously with his right fist. His nose broke with an audible snap that made Smedley wince.

Fur Boy staggered back and dropped to his knees, blood and snot smearing his upper lip. For a moment his hand twitched in the direction of his knife, then stopped when he saw the less fancy but no less lethal toothpick gripped in Fargo's fist.

"Bother anybody you want to," Fargo said, "except me. If you weren't so corned, you'd be dead right now. You've had your one break. If you even get close to me again I'll gut you."

There was no bravado in Fargo's voice, just a blunt warning. The unwashed, stinking troublemaker stared at Fargo for a few seconds to save face, then rose and staggered into the middle of the room. He had just been publicly gelded and now, by God, he sought to vent his drunken rage on an easier target.

Fargo watched the humiliated blowhard push his way toward a solitary figure leaning in a dark corner.

"You, Red Speckles! Didn't I tell you to stay clear of this place? Ain't you got no better place to cough yourself to death?"

Fargo watched the accosted man move out of the shadows. "The ass waggeth his ears."

He was dulcet-voiced and confident in the way of a cultured card cheat. Fargo took in a small, thin man who had the preternatural gleam in his eye of a consumptive. There was a morbid, ashen pallor to his skin. Obviously of spare frame, even when healthier, he had clearly lost so much weight that his cheekbones protruded, lending a ghoulish cast to his aspect. His dirty corduroy coat seemed to engulf him.

His obvious deterioration, however, didn't distract Fargo's attention from the Colt Navy in a hand-tooled, cutaway leather holster tied low on the man's right thigh—and showing clearly below the coat.

"Listen to this shit!" The drunken bully played to the crowd. "Oh, he's savage as a meat ax, ain't he? Too weak to even fuck a woman, but he's the big he-bull now, hey?"

He yanked the bowie knife out of his sash and showed off the blade. "You know, a couple exter holes in them lungs should help him breathe easier, hey, boys?"

The consumptive's unsteady hand held a pony glass of whiskey. He raised it in toast. "Here's looking at you—which is why I need this drink, shit-heel."

Fur Boy's nose hurt like hell by now, and most of the other men were mocking him. His voice yielded to brute anger.

"Swallow back that insult, you worthless cheese dick! Swallow it back!"

"As Mr. Fargo just tutored you, you should never step in something you can't wipe off. Why don't you stumble along now before I decide to kill you?"

Had Fargo blinked he would have missed it. Fur Boy took one step closer and faster than spit through a trumpet the Colt filled the consumptive's hand and spat red-orange fire.

A neat, small hole appeared in the bully's forehead, a thin worm of blood spurting out of it while a pig's-knuckle-sized clot of brain matter blew out the exit hole. Fur Boy immediately folded dead to the floor, smacking into it like a bale of newspapers.

"God's trousers!" somebody exclaimed. "*He's* feeling hot pitchforks!"

A few men cheered the entertainment—boredom could be worse than Indian attacks. For Fargo it was just one more unremarkable death among many he had either caused or witnessed: just a second or two of nerve twitching as the body tried to deny the final, certain fact of its own demise.

The consumptive's gaze caught Fargo's eye and quickly moved on, looking instead at the body.

"Break out the quicklime, Smedley! 'He has gone to seek the Great Perhaps!' "

This little burst of animation inspired laughter but also sent the consumptive into a racking spasm of coughing. When he recovered, his eyes again met Fargo's before he looked away and flipped two dollars in silver—dragging-out money—onto the corpse. He edged outside as more coughs shook his frame.

*I don't like this,* Fargo thought. *He was looking at me for a reason, and nothing good can come of it.* Fargo had seen the diseased man's face when those brains went flying, and it had all the bliss of a man taking a woman. He was the kill-crazy type, and in Fargo's experience that was the most dangerous kind. They killed on impulse.

"Welcome to Fort Pierre," Fargo told himself. "Now just keep riding."

Also in the *USA Today*
bestselling series

# *Comanche Trail:*
## *A Ralph Compton Novel*

by Carlton Stowers

Thad Taylor is no one's idea of a fine man. He's
disapproved of by most—especially his father. But
when his father doesn't return from a trip across the
Kansas plains, Thad is the only one who can search for
him. And he's far from ready for the ordeal....

Thad's father has fallen victim to the bloody
Benders—a demented family who lures travelers into
their cabin way station only to rob and brutally
murder them.

Now, in his father's memory, Thad must hunt the
Benders down and deliver them either to the law—or
to the grave.

**Available wherever books are sold or at
penguin.com**

S0539

## USA Today BESTSELLING AUTHOR
# RALPH COTTON

CROSSING FIRE RIVER
ESCAPE FROM FIRE RIVER
GUN COUNTRY
FIGHTING MEN
HANGING IN WILD WIND
BLACK VALLEY RIDERS
JUSTICE
CITY OF BAD MEN
GUN LAW
SUMMERS' HORSES
JACKPOT RIDGE
LAWMAN FROM NOGALES
SABRE'S EDGE
INCIDENT AT GUNN POINT
MIDNIGHT RIDER
WILDFIRE
LOOKOUT HILL
VALLEY OF THE GUN
BETWEEN HELL AND TEXAS
HIGH WILD DESERT
RED MOON
LAWLESS TRAIL
TWISTED HILLS
SHADOW RIVER
DARK HORSES

Available wherever books are sold or at
penguin.com

S909

*No other series packs this much heat!*

# THE TRAILSMAN

**Follow the trail of Penguin's Action Westerns at**
**penguin.com/actionwesterns**